The Time and Space of Uncle Albert

RUSSELL STANNARD

★ ☆ ★

THE TIME AND SPACE OF UNCLE ALBERT

Henry Holt and Company ★ *New York*

First published in the United States in 1990 by
Henry Holt and Company, Inc.,
115 West 18th Street, New York, New York 10011.
Published in Canada by Fitzhenry & Whiteside Limited,
195 Allstate Parkway, Markham, Ontario L3R 4T8.
Originally published in Great Britain by
Faber and Faber Limited, 3 Queen Square, London WC1N 3AU.

Library of Congress Cataloging-in-Publication Data
Stannard, Russell.
    The time and space of Uncle Albert / by Russell Stannard.
    Summary: Gedanken's eccentric uncle sends her into outer space in
a spacecraft to help him conduct a series of experiments regarding
the law of relativity as it affects time and space.
    ISBN 0-8050-1309-1
    [1. Relativity (Physics)—Fiction.   2. Uncles—Fiction.
3. Science fiction.]   I. Title.
PZ7.S79314Ti   1990
[Fic]—dc20   89-24653

Henry Holt books are available at special discounts
for bulk purchases for sales promotions, premiums,
fund-raising, or educational use. Special editions
or book excerpts can also be created to specification.

    For details contact:

    Special Sales Director
    Henry Holt and Company, Inc.
    115 West 18th Street
    New York, New York 10011

First American Edition
Designed by Victoria Hartman
Printed in the United States of America
10 9 8 7 6 5 4 3 2 1

Contents

This is a story—but no ordinary one. Although the adventures of Uncle Albert and Gedanken are make-believe, the nature of space and time really is as extraordinary as here described.

1

The Light Beam
That Got Away

"Turnip wants us to do a project," Gedanken announced.

"Turnip?" repeated Uncle Albert.

"Mr. Turner—the science teacher. We have to choose a topic—a scientific one. Then," she added with an air of importance, "we have to research it. . . ."

"Research it!" exclaimed Uncle Albert, looking as though he were going to burst out laughing.

"Yes," said Gedanken indignantly. "We have to research it—and write up the results in a folder."

Sulkily she kicked a stone—hard. She was wearing sneakers, so it hurt. But she didn't let on. She was very fond of her uncle, but he could be so annoying at times. She hoped one day to be a famous scientist like him. That's why she had hoped he would be pleased at her news. She now wished she had stayed at home and watched television.

Sensing her disappointment, Uncle Albert apologized.

"Sorry. It's just that . . . well, we didn't do that sort of thing when I was at school. What's your topic?"

Gedanken shrugged. "Haven't decided yet. Alison's doing dinosaurs. Frances Alexandra's doing something on volcanoes. Turnip says I could do 'Energy in the Home'—insulation, electric toothbrushes, and that sort of thing. But I'm not sure. I'd like to do something really interesting."

They reached the park, and Uncle Albert thankfully sat down on a bench. Gedanken joined him. Together they looked up at the sky. It was a lovely, starlit night.

"Isn't that just beautiful," began Uncle Albert. "You know, when I was a boy, I used to wonder how far away they were—the stars. I thought they were little lights stuck on to the inside of a great big dome. One night—it was just like this—I saw my dad's ladder leaning up against the wall—right up to the gutters it was. He'd been fixing them, or painting them or something—I can't remember. I climbed to the top—without him knowing, of course. I reached up as high as I could, standing on tiptoe. I tried to touch the stars—but there was nothing there. They seemed as far away as ever. I've never forgotten that."

He seemed lost in wonder at the recollection of that childhood discovery.

"How far away are they, Uncle?"

"A long way."

"But *how* far?"

"Ooh . . ." he paused, lost for words. "So far that it . . . well . . . it takes years for their light to get here."

"What?" Gedanken was not sure she had heard him correctly.

"Yes. Years. That light we're now looking at was given out years ago. It's taken that long to get here."

"But why? It doesn't take *time* for light to go from one place to another. When I put on a light at home, the light goes everywhere at the same time."

"Not quite," explained Uncle Albert. "It only *seems* to get everywhere at once. That's because rooms are small. You don't notice the tiny, tiny time it takes for the light to go from the lamp bulb to the walls. But out there in space it's different. The stars are a long, long way off, and their light takes ages to make the journey to us—and that's despite how fast it goes."

"How fast?"

"Three hundred thousand kilometers a second."

He saw her looking blank, so added, "A hundred and eighty-six thousand miles a second."

She still didn't seem to take it in.

"Five times around the Earth in the time it takes to say 'rice pudding.' "

"Five times . . . ?"

"That's right. That's how fast it goes. And it still takes years to get here from those stars even at that speed."

They continued to sit there gazing up at the sky, lost in thought.

Suddenly Uncle Albert sat bolt upright and exclaimed, "I've had an idea! I've been wondering lately about light—how it behaves, and what it would be like actually to catch up with a beam of light—one of those beams of starlight up there, for example. Yes, of course. Why didn't I think of it before? How about you giving me a hand? You go and chase one of those beams and then tell me what it's like."

Gedanken looked at him suspiciously. She had heard people say he was "eccentric." She didn't quite know what they meant by that, but it sounded as though they thought he was a bit odd. There were times—like this—when she thought they might have a point.

"Are you all right, Uncle?" she inquired anxiously.

"All right? Of course I am," he exclaimed, springing to his feet with surprising agility. "Come on. We've got work to do." And with that he started hurrying off in the direction of the house.

"But, Uncle, I don't understand," protested Gedanken, catching up with him. "How am I supposed to do it? You've just said that light travels so fast that . . ."

"I'll show you," he said, interrupting her. "In fact, this could be your project. How about that? A piece of real, genuine research. Ha!" he snorted. "That'll show old Turnip and his electric toothbrushes." With that, he grabbed her hand and eagerly pulled her along.

By the time they got home, Gedanken was thoroughly exasperated. Uncle Albert still hadn't explained what was going on. As he took off his coat and was about to enter his study, Gedanken planted herself firmly in front of the door.

"You're not going another step until you answer my question," she insisted. "How am I to do it?"

"In a spacecraft, of course," said Uncle Albert, as though it were obvious.

"A spacecraft. You want me to chase a beam of light in a spacecraft?"

"Yes."

"Ha, ha," she said mockingly. "Now pull the other one."

"Eh?"

"Well, let's face it, you haven't got one, have you?"

"Haven't I?" he asked with amusement.

As he brushed past her, he beckoned her to follow him.

"But I don't for one moment believe . . ."

As they entered the study, her voice trailed off, her eyes opened wide. She stood rooted to the floor in astonishment.

"What on earth . . . ?"

The room was dimly lit by the embers of a fire and by a desk lamp that had been left on. The walls were lined with books. On either side of the fireplace were two comfortable, well-worn leather armchairs.

It was something above one of these armchairs that had caught Gedanken's attention. It was like a gigantic soap bubble. About a yard across, it was almost spherical but slightly squashed at the top and bottom. Beneath it, to one side, were two smaller bubbles that reached down toward the top of the high-backed chair. They wobbled gently and glinted mysteriously in the half-light.

"What is that?" she exclaimed.

"That? Er . . . it's a thought-bubble," Uncle Albert said in a matter-of-fact tone.

"A what?"

"Thought-bubble. You know . . . thought-bubbles, like you get in cartoons. Things that go over people's heads when they think."

"But you only get those in comics. I didn't know they were . . . well . . . real."

"Not surprised. There aren't many of them. Not many people think hard enough to produce one."

Uncle Albert sat down in the chair under the bubble and waved Gedanken to sit in the chair opposite him. She did so, still looking up at the bubble uncertainly.

As she watched it, it seemed to fade away at times and then to brighten up again.

"Why does it go and come back like that?"

"Depends on how hard I am thinking."

"What . . ." Gedanken paused, not quite sure what question she wanted to ask. "What does it . . . do?"

"Anything. It can do anything. All it requires is imagination. Lots and lots of imagination. Whatever I think of comes up there in the thought-bubble. Tell you what," he added. "You watch."

He closed his eyes. To Gedanken's delight, in no time at all a black-and-white cat began slowly to come into view in the bubble. It looked incredibly real. As she watched, it began to lick its fur. It then looked up, winked at her—and disappeared.

Uncle Albert opened his eyes. "Did you see it?"

"Yes," said Gedanken excitedly. "It was . . . well . . . just like a *real* cat. It's amazing."

Uncle Albert grinned.

"Tell me, Uncle," she said, "if you thought of *me*, would I end up in the thought-bubble?"

Uncle Albert thought for a moment. "I reckon so. I've never tried it out on real people before. But I think it would work."

"And if you thought of a spacecraft?"

Uncle Albert nodded.

"And what if you thought of me being in the spacecraft . . . ?"

"Exactly. That's what I guess would happen. You'd get beamed up into the spacecraft. You'd then be able to chase the light beam for me."

He looked at her intently. "Gedanken, I've no right to ask you this. But as I've told you, I've been trying to understand the behavior of light. I've got stuck. I can't fathom it out. I need someone to chase a light beam for me and tell me what it's like when you catch up with it. I can't go myself—I have to stay here doing the thinking. So I was hoping . . ."

Gedanken's heart was pounding. She looked anxiously at the bubble and gripped the arms of her chair. Then she looked across at Uncle Albert. "Is it . . . well . . . dangerous?" she asked.

Uncle Albert shrugged. "Shouldn't have thought so. But as I said, I've never done this before to a real person."

She thought for a moment, then nodded timidly. Uncle Albert smiled reassuringly at her.

"Okay, then," he said. "Here goes."

He closed his eyes, rested his chin in his hand, and his face became concentrated in thought.

As Gedanken watched, there began to materialize in the bubble what looked like the interior of a space-craft. There were curved metal walls, and set into them were round windows. Outside the windows she caught a glimpse of stars. Close by was an imposing array of dials, winking lights, and TV screens. This was presumably the control panel.

Suddenly a rush of panic seized her. The bubble! Where was the bubble? It had gone. She had become so wrapped up in thinking about what was inside the bubble that she hadn't noticed that the bubble itself had disappeared.

Not only that, but the chair arms she was gripping were no longer those of the armchair in Uncle Albert's study; they were the arms of a seat in a spacecraft. In a flash she realized that somehow—incredibly—she was now *inside* the thought-bubble. And not only in the thought-bubble—she was in a spacecraft!

She looked wildly about her. There was only one

thought in her mind: Where was the exit? But before she could move, a voice boomed out.

"Hello there. Don't be alarmed, my dear. Nothing to worry about." It had an artificial, electronic sound about it.

"What . . . what's going on?" stammered Gedanken, trying to identify the source of the voice.

"Allow me to introduce myself. I am your computer. And it is my pleasure to welcome you aboard. I hope you had a pleasant trip up here."

She noticed some lights that winked on and off in time to the sound of the voice, and also a nearby screen that displayed the words as they were spoken. This must be a talking computer.

"But where am I?" she asked, feeling a bit foolish talking to a TV screen.

"Why, you are in the spacecraft, of course."

"I'm actually in a spacecraft?"

"Not *a* spacecraft, if you don't mind," said the computer coldly. "This is *the* spacecraft." Then, in a voice that sounded like a guide addressing a large group of tourists, it continued, "This is the largest spacecraft that has never been built and never will be. . . ."

"Well, if it's never been built, how come it's here?" interrupted Gedanken, somewhat gaining in courage.

"By the power of thought, of course—Uncle Albert's imagination. There are no limits to what he can imagine. Now where was I? Ah, yes," the computer resumed. "This is the world's largest spacecraft. It is equipped with the most powerful rocket engine ever devised—capable of delivering all the energy one could possibly require. The spacecraft is designed to explore the laws of nature to their ultimate limits."

Gedanken looked about her. The spacecraft was certainly *huge*. It was like being in a vast, long tunnel. The far end was so distant, she could hardly make it out at all. As for the computer, it sounded a bit pompous, but she was grateful to have someone—anyone—to talk to—even if it was only a pile of electronics.

"All right, madam," the computer started up again. "It's my pleasure to be the first to congratulate you."

"Congratulate me?"

"To congratulate you on becoming the first captain of this fine craft."

Gedanken was overcome—at first. But then she panicked again.

"But there must be some mistake. I don't know the first thing about spacecrafts. I wouldn't know what to do."

"Not to worry. What do you think I'm here for? It's my job to look after you and see that everything runs smoothly. All you have to do is . . . well . . . just enjoy it. All right. Are you ready?"

Gedanken looked happier and nodded.

"Okay. Strap yourself in."

She fastened her seat belt.

"Now, all you have to worry about is that red button in front of you. When you want to start up the motor, you just press the button. Keep your finger on it for as long as you want the rocket to fire. All right?"

"Yes." She nodded, getting more and more excited.

"Okay. When you're ready, you can blast off."

Gedanken took a deep breath, reached out, and pressed the button. Immediately from the rear of the spacecraft there came a throaty roar of engine noise. She felt herself flattened against the back of the seat.

How thrilling! she thought.

After a while the computer called out, "You can let go of the button when you like."

She did so, and the engine noise died away. No longer was she pressed against her seat. She had a floating sensation and felt she would go drifting off if the seat belt hadn't continued to hold her in position. It was very pleasant once one got used to it.

"That's our speed, is it?" asked Gedanken, pointing to a digital readout just above the button in front of her. It said SPEED RELATIVE TO EARTH and was reading "0.500 times the speed of light."

"That's right," said the computer. "We're now traveling at half the speed of light."

"Then why aren't we slowing down?"

"Why should we?"

"Because the engine's off. We ought to be slowing down."

"This is not a bicycle," the computer said in a superior tone of voice. "This is a spacecraft. Once a spacecraft is up to speed, it doesn't need pushing anymore. Out here there is no air or anything to slow us down. So we just keep cruising along. We only need the rocket motor when we want to *change* speed—when we want to go faster or slower."

"How does a motor make you go slower?"

"By going into reverse, of course."

Above the digital readout was a large window facing out of the front of the spacecraft. Gedanken looked at the stars laid out before her. With each moment she was feeling more relaxed and at home. She was really beginning to enjoy it all.

"All right," interrupted the computer. "If you're ready, we had better get on with our mission. Uncle Albert has programmed some instructions into me somewhere. I'll have a look in my memory bank."

"We're to catch up with a light beam," Gedanken volunteered eagerly.

There was a pause, and the computer resumed, "Ah, yes. Quite right. Catch a light beam, he says. How peculiar. Suppose he knows what he's doing. All right, can you see one? There ought to be plenty about with all those stars out there."

Gedanken peered out of the window. Suddenly she pointed excitedly. "There! Is that one?"

Directly outside, a shimmering glow sped by. It seemed to Gedanken to have a face—an impish face . . . and . . . yes, it was giggling! She definitely heard a faint, high-pitched giggle, like an overexcited schoolgirl, and a teasing voice that called, "Go on. Catch me if you can." As it got farther away, the fuzzy light patch got smaller and fainter.

"Yes!" cried the computer. "That's one. After it, before it gets away!"

"Easy!" shouted Gedanken. "We're already doing half its speed." And with that she pressed the button, the engines roared into life once more, and they were giving chase.

After a few minutes the computer called out, "Okay. That should do it. We ought to have caught up with it by now."

Gedanken released the button and looked for the light beam. Her face fell.

"Oh. It's farther away than ever," she said.

"What? Farther away. . . . That's impossible."

"But it is."

"Can't be. What speed are we doing?" asked the computer.

"Er . . . zero point nine zero zero. Nine-tenths the speed of light—I think."

"Is that all?"

"Yes," she confirmed.

"How odd. According to my calculations, we ought easily to be doing the speed of light."

Gedanken heard a far-off voice giggling and laughing: "You'll have to do better than that."

"Give it another go," said the computer. "I'll put you on full power this time."

Gedanken pressed the button again. The engine noise was deafening—far louder than before. The spacecraft shuddered and shook in a most alarming manner. It was as though it were about to shatter into tiny pieces.

After what seemed an age, the computer instructed her to let go of the button, and she thankfully did so.

She peered out of the window. At first she could see nothing. Then she spotted the light beam.

"Oh, no. It's miles away now—and it's still going away from us."

"Impossible. What's our speed now?"

"Zero point nine nine nine times the speed of light."

"Most irregular. The answer I've got is quite different." Then, with a note of disgust in its voice, it added, "I must have been misprogrammed. I've heard of this sort of thing. Never thought it would happen to me, though. How embarrassing. I'll have to do a check on myself."

". . . can't wait . . . can't wait . . . must be on my way . . ."

Gedanken heard the light beam's voice dying away in the distance. The fuzzy patch of light faded—and finally disappeared. *How am I going to explain this to Uncle Albert when I get back?* Gedanken thought. *And bang goes my project into the bargain.*

Then, with a rising sense of unease, she continued aloud, "In fact, *how* am I going to get back? Here I am flying about at light speeds—and the only help I've got is a stupid computer that can't do its times tables."

"Aha!" cried the computer. "It's all right. It's not a programming error. Everything is working properly. I've been working things out exactly as I was told to."

"Then how did you get the wrong answer?"

"The wrong answer?"

"Yes. The wrong answer for our speed."

"Ah. Yes. I see what you mean. Good question . . . the wrong speed . . . hmmm . . . I suppose I must have been fed the wrong equation. I have been working things out correctly—as I always do—but with the wrong equation. That must be it. The actual scientific equation must be wrong. How very strange. I wonder what Uncle Albert will make of that. You'll have to tell him when you get back."

"I *am* going to get back all right, aren't I?" asked Gedanken anxiously. "You know, with you doing your equations wrong . . ."

"I beg your pardon!" exclaimed the computer, sounding very cross.

"I'm sorry. I meant to say . . . well . . . with things being the way you said they were . . . am I going to be all right?"

"Oh, yes. No problem. I'll send a message to him right away to say that you're ready to be beamed down." And sure enough, there was no problem. As mysteriously as Gedanken had found herself transported up to the spacecraft, so she now found herself back in the reassuring atmosphere of Uncle Albert's study. She immediately told him everything that had happened. ". . . And there's nothing more to say," she ended. "We did our best, but the light beam was too fast for us." She shrugged her shoulders.

"Don't you worry, my girl," said Uncle Albert. In fact, he was looking quite pleased with himself. "As far as I'm concerned, everything has worked out very nicely. Drink up your cocoa before it gets cold. You ought to be on your way home in a few minutes."

Gedanken picked up the mug from the small table

by the side of her chair. She had on previous occasions mentioned that she was not all that crazy about cocoa, but as usual Uncle Albert had forgotten.

"What do you mean, it's worked out very nicely? I'm not going to be able to write about it in my project. And it was your idea in the first place that I should go chasing it. So aren't you disappointed too?"

"Disappointed? Not a bit. You see, I couldn't for the life of me imagine what it would be like to catch up with a light beam. That's why I had gotten stuck. So it's quite a relief that you didn't manage to."

"I thought you were able to imagine anything at all," said Gedanken.

"Oh, no. I don't let my imagination run away with me. I only imagine what might be possible. I don't waste time thinking of things that are absolutely impossible." He paused, searching for words.

"Light is very special, Gedanken. It's always rushing about. And I do mean always. It just can't keep still. It's the way it's made. Its movement is part of what it *is*."

"Like dancing."

"Dancing?"

"Yes. You move when you're dancing. If you're standing still on one spot, you can't be dancing."

"Well . . . yes. I hadn't thought of it like that. I suppose you're right; it is a bit like that."

"So?"

"So if you had managed to catch up with the light beam, it wouldn't have been rushing about anymore—not as far as you were concerned. It would just have sat there doing nothing."

"Don't get it."

"Well, you know what it's like when you're in a car on the highway and you catch up with another car in the next lane. You're both going fast, but it doesn't seem like it. The other car looks as though it's standing still next to you."

"Yes, I know that. So what's wrong with the same thing happening when we catch up with a light beam? Why can't we see that as if it's standing still?"

"Ah, but that's the point—with a car we know what it's like when it's standing still. Cars spend most of their time standing still—in garages and parking lots. But with light—it's different. There is no such thing as light that stands still. It's always lively, vibrating, going places. Light standing still wouldn't be light anymore. Like those dancers of yours. If they looked to you as though they were standing still, they wouldn't be dancing anymore—not as far as you were concerned. Light never stands still, so it can never *look* as though it's standing still."

"But it *will* look as though it's standing still if we catch up with it," insisted Gedanken.

"If, my dear. *If!*" exclaimed Uncle Albert. "That's what I'm getting at. We *can't* catch up with it. That's what you've just found out for me. And because we can't catch up with it, we never do see light looking as though it is standing still. It's amazing. Beautiful! Why hasn't anyone thought of it before!"

With that, he triumphantly punched the air like a soccer player scoring a goal. (He always did get excited when a Big Thought hit him.) "We're going to have to rewrite all the science books!"

Gedanken waited for him to calm down a bit.

"But what if we got a bigger rocket?"

"A bigger one? No, no, my dear, that won't do. Won't do at all. Don't you remember what the computer told you? The engine was able to deliver all the power you could possibly want."

"But this doesn't make sense. There's no air up there or anything to slow us down. Right? So what keeps us from going faster?"

Uncle Albert thought for a moment. He looked around at the desk and said, "Pass me that notepad and I'll explain."

Gedanken went and fetched it.

"Now pass me the writing desk."

She turned and was about to go back, but stopped.

"Uncle!"

"Hmmm?"

"You said the writing desk."

"That's right."

"But I can't pass you the writing desk."

"Whyever not? You passed the notepad."

"Oh, don't be silly, Uncle. You know perfectly well I can't pass *that*. It's much too heavy," she protested.

"Aha," said Uncle Albert with a tricky look in his eye. "The same girl who was strong enough to pass me a notepad wasn't strong enough to move the desk. And the reason was that the desk was much heavier."

"Yes. So? What's that got to do with the spacecraft not going faster?"

"I'm explaining! It's simple. The rocket motor pushed on the space capsule and got it to start moving. As the capsule went faster, the same rocket, pushing just as hard as before, had less effect. And when the capsule was traveling at almost the speed of light, the motor had hardly any effect at all. And it was still pushing just as hard. Why?"

Gedanken thought for a moment. "You're not saying . . ." Her voice trailed off.

"Go on," said Uncle Albert encouragingly.

"Are you saying that the capsule got *heavier* the faster it went?" she ventured. "It was like starting out pushing a notepad and ending up pushing a writing desk?"

Uncle Albert nodded.

"But why should a space capsule behave like that?" she asked. "What's so special about space capsules?"

"There's nothing special about them. *Anything* that goes really fast must get heavier. Not only the capsule, but everything on board got heavier."

"Everything? How about . . . me?"

"Yes. Even you."

"*I* got heavier?"

"That's right."

She looked down at her wrist. "But I didn't notice myself getting fat."

Uncle Albert chuckled. "No, no, it wasn't a case of putting on weight. You didn't gain extra layers of fat or anything like that. Your body was still made out of its usual stuff. It's just that the faster you went, the harder it became to push you and make you go along faster."

"But I didn't *feel* heavier," she persisted. "In fact,

quite the opposite. When the motor was off, I felt weightless. If it wasn't for the seat belt, I'd have gone floating around—like the astronauts on TV."

"Ah, but that's something different. Normally we get pulled down by gravity. . . ."

"Gravity?"

"Yes." Uncle Albert held out the notepad. "Like this. . . ." He let go of it and it fell to the floor. "Gravity did that. Gravity pulls everything down—us, for instance. But the reason we don't fall like that notepad is that the surface of the Earth is pushing up on us. . . ."

"It's not pushing up on me," said Gedanken, looking down at her feet. Because the chair she was sitting in was too big for her, her feet were not quite touching the floor.

Uncle Albert laughed. "True. In your case, it's the seat of the chair pushing up on your bottom that keeps you from falling. Anyway, the reason you normally feel heavy is that gravity is pulling you down at the same time as something is pushing you up."

"And how is it different up there in the spacecraft?"

"Up there you were floating freely. The seat of the spacecraft wasn't pushing up on you, so you didn't feel heavy. But when it came to pushing on you to try and make you go faster, then it was like trying to push something that was heavy, and the faster you went, the heavier you seemed to get."

"How very peculiar," murmured Gedanken, thinking to herself that whatever else got heavy, this conversation was becoming a bit heavy-going.

Uncle Albert got up and started to clear away the mugs. "It's time you were going. Your mother will be wondering what's happened. As for me, I've got to think about this discovery of yours. We shall need a new scientific law—one that says things get heavier with greater speeds."

Gedanken rose and followed him into the kitchen. She took the mugs from him and started to rinse them out.

"Why does this only happen when we get close to the speed of light?"

"Hmmm. I suppose it doesn't. I suppose this *always* happens. Every time we go faster, it's as though we get heavier."

"Well, why haven't people noticed it before?"

"I can only think that in normal everyday life—at ordinary speeds—the effect must be too small to be measured."

"How about when you travel in an express train?"

"No, it would still be too small to notice."

"A supersonic airplane? The space shuttle?"

"No, not even those. The effect will be there. It must always be there. But it's only when you make the kind of space journey you've just made, and travel almost as fast as light does, that it becomes noticeable."

"Tell me, Uncle. How heavy did I become?"

"Well, when you were going at half the speed of light, you would have been about ten pounds heavier. Then, at nine-tenths the speed of light, you would have been twice as heavy as normal. And toward the end . . . well, it's hard to say, the digital readout ran out of nines, but it wouldn't surprise me if you got as heavy as Buckingham Palace."

"Buckingham Palace?" she exclaimed in wide-eyed astonishment.

Uncle Albert nodded.

"Amazing," she breathed.

She got as far as the back door. She kissed Uncle Albert on the forehead and turned to go out—but stopped. A thought had struck her.

"I say, Uncle. You know I was going to do a project on what it's like to catch up with a light beam. Well, now that we know we can't catch up with it, why don't I do one on *why* we can't? I could tell them all this stuff about getting heavier."

"That's a good idea. In fact, a very good idea."

What a funny sort of evening, thought Gedanken as she lay tucked up in bed. It's a good thing there was nothing on television—I might have missed it all.

For a moment she thought she saw the little light beams from her bedside lamp. They seemed to be chasing each other across the room to see who could get to the other side first.

In a way I still wish I could have caught up with that beam of starlight, she thought. But then, it's not everyone who can say they once weighed as much as Buckingham Palace. I wonder if I'll get in the *Guiness Book of World Records*.

She yawned, reached out, and switched off the lamp. Old Turnip's going to get a surprise, she thought. Then, But what if he doesn't believe it all. . . .

In no time she was fast asleep.

2

★ ☆ ★

The Watch That Went Slow—But Kept Good Time

T here was a ring at the back door. Uncle Albert stopped peeling the potatoes, wiped his wet hands on the sides of his trousers, and answered it.

"Ah, good morning, Gedanken," he said. "Or should I say, 'Happy birthday,' my dear!"

"Thank you, Uncle," replied Gedanken, stepping inside. "I wondered whether you would remember what day it was."

"Remember? Of course I remember! I know I'm getting forgetful, but I'm not *that* bad. Even have a present for you somewhere—I think."

He turned and started rummaging through drawers and cupboards, among the cookbooks, in the wash basket, and behind the refrigerator. After what seemed an age he gave a triumphant cry, "Ah, there it is!" and pulled out a small, slim package. It had been jammed at the back of the cutlery drawer.

"What is it?" asked Gedanken, hardly able to wait.

"You'd better open it and find out."

Gedanken quickly tore off the pretty wrapping paper, thinking as she did how thoughtful Uncle Albert had been to wrap it so nicely for her. She opened the box. It contained a digital watch.

"Uncle!" she exclaimed delightedly. "However did you know that's what I wanted? It's *exactly* what I wanted. You must be psychic."

"I wouldn't have thought so. I have a tongue in my head, don't I?"

"What do you mean?" asked Gedanken, looking puzzled. Then she added, "Oh, I see. You asked Mum and Dad."

Uncle Albert set the watch to the right time for her and showed her how to alter the date. She put it on her wrist.

"It keeps very good time," he said. "It'll gain or lose only a few seconds each month."

"Why does it say 'Quartz' on the front?"

"That's what helps it to keep time. Inside there's a tiny crystal of quartz. It's connected with an electrical circuit that helps govern how fast the watch runs. It's the same as what happens in the digital clock in my study," he said. "I swear by it. Never known it to be wrong by more than a few seconds."

Gedanken was thrilled and gave her uncle a big hug.

"So what are you going to do with your day?" he asked. "Why aren't you at school?"

"It's Saturday—what did you think?"

"Oh, yes, I forgot."

"Don't know what I'm going to do. There's a dance tonight, of course."

"Where's that going to be?" asked Uncle Albert, turning back to the potatoes in the sink.

"At home."

"At home? Your poor parents."

"They said they might be going out. I hope they do," she added, looking a little concerned. "It would be awful if they stayed. They'd ruin everything. They'd make us keep the music down. Still," she continued, brightening up, "Nick Jordan said he might come."

"Nick Jordan? Who's he?"

"Ohhh, just one of the boys in my class."

"Just one of the boys?" inquired Uncle Albert with a knowing look.

"We-ell, you know . . ." said Gedanken, a little awkwardly. "All the girls are after him, and he did say he might come when I asked him, and he's never said yes before—to anyone. He's got a strobe light and heaps of records—he said he might bring them with him."

"Well, let's keep our fingers crossed," said Uncle Albert gravely.

Gedanken smiled. "Stop teasing, Uncle."

He put the saucepan on the stove. "All right, that's ready for later. So . . . you're all sorted out for this evening. By the way, how's the project going?"

"I was just about to come to that." She looked at him questioningly. "I was wondering . . ."

"Yes?"

"Well, I was just wondering—seeing that it's my birthday and all that . . ."

"Yes?" asked Uncle Albert a little impatiently. "Get on with it."

"Well, I was wondering whether I could go for another ride in the spacecraft—just a short one." She added, "It *might* help with the project."

"Oh?" said Uncle Albert, looking interested. "What do you have in mind?"

"Well, I'm not really sure," she said uncertainly. "But it might help."

"Meaning that it's your birthday, and birthdays are all about having treats, and doing exactly what you like, and people making a fuss over you as though they have nothing better to do with their time, and you enjoyed your last ride so why shouldn't you go again."

"Well, I didn't mean it like that. . . ." said Gedanken a little shamefacedly.

"Whyever not? That's what *I've* always thought birthdays were about." He started toward the door of his study and indicated with a slight movement of the head that she should follow. "Where to? Fancy a trip to the moon?"

Gedanken's eyes widened. "That would be wonderful!" she exclaimed.

"Could probably throw in the odd planet, too, if you like."

"Yes, please," she said as she hurried after him, ready to be beamed up again to the spacecraft.

"In a few moments we shall be landing on the moon. Please fasten your seat belts, extinguish cigarettes, and have your seats in the upright position. We shall be staying here for half an hour. Passengers wishing to disembark are reminded that because of the lack of atmosphere they should wear space suits."

Why the computer insisted on talking in this way Gedanken could not understand. Anyone would think that the spacecraft was filled with package-tour vacationers—instead of Gedanken being on her own.

"Passengers on the right-hand side of the craft will see out of the window a flag. We are landing right near the place where the astronauts came some years ago."

The retrorocket engine fired. There was a bump. The engine switched off. They had arrived.

In great excitement Gedanken clumped down the steel ladder in her bulky space suit and stepped onto the ground. She was standing on the moon!

Imagine me being here, she thought.

She jumped up and down and marveled at how high she could go. Then she remembered the TV pictures of the astronauts doing the same thing—something to do with gravity being lower on the moon than on the Earth.

Then she caught sight of the little car the astronauts had used for their longer explorations—the moon buggy. Gedanken wondered whether by any chance it still worked. She went over to it and climbed aboard. She looked at the instrument panel. There was a button marked STARTER. She pressed it,

but nothing happened. Then she pulled it. Immediately she felt the engine shudder uncertainly. Then, to her delight, it settled down and the car began to move forward.

She was off. Chasing around, swerving this way and that, bouncing high in the air (except that there wasn't any) and sending up clouds of dust.

"Would passengers please return to the spacecraft. We are about to depart," boomed the voice of the computer coming from somewhere inside her helmet. It must be a radio link, she thought.

Back she went. As she settled down into her seat again, she heard a funny slithering noise. Suddenly a large bar of chocolate shot out of an opening in the electronic panel of the computer and landed in her lap.

"Happy birthday, Gedanken," said the computer. "I thought you might be needing this."

Gedanken smiled. "That's very kind of you, Mr. Computer."

With that, the spacecraft soared upward on the second part of its journey.

Next they visited Mars, a planet half the size of the Earth. It looked to be a wild place, with craters, canyons, and vast sheets of ice. The surface was being continuously swept by fierce dust storms. Gedanken was disappointed to learn that there were definitely no such things as Martians down there.

"What a pity. I thought I was going to meet one," she said.

They skipped the planet Venus.

"Nasty, horrid place," said the computer. "Hot as molten lead and covered in dirty yellow clouds of acid."

They also crossed Mercury off their list.

"Another nasty place," explained the computer. "Much too close to the sun. Get fried alive if we landed there."

Instead, they headed out to the giant planets Jupiter and Saturn. Jupiter was huge—ten times the diameter of the Earth. It was a mass of swirling white-and-orange clouds lit by vivid flashes of lightning. (It reminded Gedanken a little of Nick Jordan's strobe light.) Jupiter had no fewer than four moons about the size of Earth's, as well as some much smaller ones. One of the bigger moons was multicolored, and Gedanken could see at least half a dozen volcanoes erupting violently, throwing out blazing hot lava.

But most spectacular of all was Saturn. Gedanken just couldn't get over the sheer beauty and splendor of its rings—giant flattened disks encircling the planet.

"Whatever are they?" she asked.

"Dust and rocks," replied the computer. "Just dust and rocks."

She would have liked to have visited the remaining three planets, Uranus, Neptune, and Pluto, but the computer said they were too far away to be reached on a half-day excursion, so they turned and made their way home.

"That was wonderful," said Gedanken when she got back to Uncle Albert's study. "I can't wait to tell everyone at the dance tonight."

"Shouldn't bother if I were you," said Uncle Albert. "They'll never believe you."

They both laughed.

"Well, it *was* wonderful all the same," she insisted. "But I must say that of all the places we visited, I still think the Earth is the nicest place to live."

"Couldn't agree more. Now off you go, or you'll be late for your lunch."

Gedanken looked across at the digital clock on the mantelpiece over the fireplace. She looked puzzled.

"Is that the clock you were telling me about, Uncle? The one that's always supposed to keep the right time?"

"Yes. Why?"

"Well, it's wrong. Either that, or my watch is wrong."

"Wrong?"

"Yes. That says two o'clock; mine says five to one. I hope it's *not* two o'clock or I'll be in trouble with Mum. She told me I was to be back at one."

"Oh, dear, I'm sorry," said Uncle Albert. "Time just seems to fly these days. I hadn't noticed. It certainly is two o'clock."

"But it simply can't be that late," Gedanken insisted.

"I'll check if you like," said Uncle Albert, going over to the telephone and dialing for the time.

". . . At the tone the time will be two oh three and ten seconds, exactly. . . . *Beep* . . . At the tone . . ."

"Yes, it's two o'clock all right," he said.

"So my watch *is* slow then," said Gedanken unhappily.

"But . . ." began Uncle Albert. "It can't be slow. It's a quartz one. Here, give it to me."

He took it and held it next to the digital clock and watched the two pulsing away.

"No," he said, "as far as I can tell, they seem to be keeping pace with each other okay. Leave it with me. I'll have a look at it. I must have set it wrong in the first place."

"No, Uncle. You didn't," said Gedanken. "I noticed when you were doing it. You set it to the right time all right."

"I did?" murmured Uncle Albert, looking very puzzled. "Hmmm."

He wandered over to the study window and looked up at the sky outside. "I wonder. . . . I just wonder. . . ."

"You wonder what, Uncle?"

"Uh? Oh, nothing, nothing."

But Gedanken knew that something was up. She was sure she detected a Think coming on. In fact, she could just make out the thought-bubble appearing once more over Uncle Albert's chair.

"Off you go," he said gruffly. "You're late. Tell your mother it's my fault. Yes, tell her it's my fault. I should have realized."

"Realized *what*?" insisted Gedanken.

"Nothing," said Uncle Albert firmly. "Run along with you. But . . ."

"But what, Uncle?"

He smiled. "But hurry back this afternoon—we've got more work to do."

There was a ring at the back door. It was Gedanken. To Uncle Albert it seemed she hadn't been away more than five minutes.

"What?" exclaimed Uncle Albert. "Eaten your lunch already? You'll get indigestion."

"Didn't want to miss anything," she said eagerly as she came inside, looking about her expectantly.

"Well," she said. "What are we going to do?"

"Well, it's like this," said Uncle Albert. "I've been thinking . . ."

"I knew it."

"This morning, when you went on that journey, how fast did you go?"

"Don't know. Wasn't noticing. Except on the way back. We got pretty close to the speed limit then because I knew I had to be back by one o'clock."

"The speed limit?"

"Yes. The speed of light. . . . We can't go as fast . . ."

"Oh, I see what you mean," said Uncle Albert with a smile. Then he added thoughtfully, "So you did get up close to the speed of light. I thought you must have."

"Why?"

"Well, we've already discovered one peculiar thing that happens when we get close to the speed of light. . . ."

"We get heavier. I know. I've written it up for my project. So?"

"Well, I reckon we're on to something else. Something else peculiar."

"What?"

"Something to do with time."

"Time?" repeated Gedanken with a frown.

"Yes," said Uncle Albert. He was clearly beginning to get excited. "You see, we all assume that time is the same for everybody. When I say that something takes an hour, then I mean the same as when you say that something takes an hour; an hour here on

Earth is the same as an hour in a space capsule. But—it might not be. We don't know for sure. They might be—different."

"But that would be terribly confusing," protested Gedanken. "We can't have everyone having their own times. We wouldn't know where we were. It would be one time according to one person and . . ."

". . . and another according to someone else?" added Uncle Albert. "Perhaps five to one according to one person and two o'clock for someone else?"

Gedanken looked at him suspiciously. "You're pulling my leg. You can't be serious."

"Oh, yes, I am," said Uncle Albert. "While you were at lunch, I checked on your watch, and it's perfectly okay—just as I thought. I reset it, and it's still in sync with my clock."

He took her into the study and showed her the clock and the watch. Sure enough, they agreed exactly.

"Well, if you are serious . . . If . . ." said Gedanken. "What do you want me to do?"

"I want you to go for another ride in the spacecraft. This time I want you to leave your watch here and take my digital clock with you."

She looked puzzled. "You want me to take the clock this time . . . instead of my watch?"

"Yes, that's right. That way we'll check out whether it really was something to do with the effect of high speed on time and not something peculiar about your watch."

"So because it's the clock going at high speed, it'll

be the clock that ends up going slower than the watch this time?"

"Exactly. And not only that, I want you to take this bedroom alarm clock with you as well. It's not like the other; it doesn't depend on a quartz crystal—it's just an ordinary mechanical one. That will make sure that what we're dealing with isn't just something to do with the behavior of quartz and electrical circuits and that sort of thing."

Leaving the watch on the desktop, Uncle Albert gave the two clocks to Gedanken. Holding them carefully, she sat down opposite Uncle Albert.

As the thought-bubble began to materialize above his head, he continued, "This is what I want you to do: I want you to get up to a speed of . . . well, let's say something like nine-tenths the speed of light. Then cruise at that speed directly to Jupiter. The computer will show you the way."

"Right."

"Then, as soon as you get there, turn around and head straight back home at the same speed as before: nine-tenths the speed of light. No hanging around at the other end. You come straight back. Is that understood?"

"Understood."

"Fine. Now, we're both agreed that the time is two forty-five P.M., yes?"

"Yes," said Gedanken, comparing the readings on her two clocks with the watch on the desk. "Two forty-five, exactly."

"Okay. Off you go, and good luck."

★ ☆ ★

Everything went according to plan.

"Done it!" Gedanken announced as soon as she knew she was back in the study. "Mission completed."

"Splendid!" beamed Uncle Albert.

"I did just what you said. And here are your clocks. They both say three twenty-five P.M. It took just twenty minutes to get there and twenty minutes back."

"Twenty there and twenty back, eh?" said Uncle Albert. "Making forty minutes in all . . . and you started at two forty-five P.M. . . . So that takes us to three twenty-five, right?"

He looked over toward the desk, at Gedanken's watch. "Okay. What do you make of that?"

It read 4:15 P.M.!

"But that's not right," stated Gedanken. "I know it can't be that late. The watch must have been going too fast. It was too slow this morning and now it's too fast."

Uncle Albert got up, went over to the telephone, dialed a number, and held up the receiver for Gedanken to hear.

"At the tone the time will be four fifteen and twenty seconds, exactly. . . . *Beep* . . . At the tone . . ."

"Convinced?" he asked.

"No. No, I'm not," she replied defiantly. "You're trying to tell me I've been away for . . . well, how long is it? . . . An hour and a half. But I haven't. That's *stupid*. I just know I haven't been away that long. This time I was concentrating. I was watching those clocks the whole time. If I had been away for an hour and a half, they would have been ticking at half their normal rate—half what they're doing now—which is ridiculous. I would have noticed. I really would, Uncle. I promise. They were *not* going slow."

"All right, all right, Gedanken," soothed Uncle Albert. "I'm not denying anything you say. I'm sure you watched the clocks carefully, and I take your word for it that they appeared to you to behave perfectly normally. But I did the same thing while you were away; I sat here keeping an eye on the watch. And as far as I am concerned, it too appeared to behave normally."

"Then why do they end up reading differently?"

"Well, there is only one explanation: Time in the spacecraft is not the same as time on Earth. The journey took forty minutes of 'spacecraft time,' and an hour and a half of 'Earth-time.' "

"What *are* you talking about? Spacecraft-time and Earth-time. There's only *one* time: *the* time."

"Apparently not. There were two times. The journey took an hour and a half of Earth-time and about half that—forty minutes—of spacecraft-time. That is what you have just discovered for me."

"I don't get it," said Gedanken, looking confused. "Why did the clocks *look* as though they were normal if really they weren't?"

"But it's not just the clocks that were going slow in the spacecraft. *Everything* was going slow in the spacecraft. It's *time itself* that was slowed down. Everything. Your breathing was slowed down, your heartbeat, the rate at which you digested that lunch you bolted, your thinking . . ."

"My thinking?"

"Why, yes, of course," said Uncle Albert. "Everything happening inside the capsule was governed by spacecraft-time, and that includes the rate at which you thought about things."

"So you're saying that I was looking at clocks that were going slow, but with a brain that was also going slow."

"That's right."

"And my brain was slowed down by the same amount as the things I was looking at—the clocks, my breathing rate, and everything?"

"Yes. Your clocks were going at half their normal rate, but you were looking at them with a brain that was also going at half its normal rate—so everything looked normal."

"Amazing."

He grinned. "Yes. That should make quite an eye-opening chapter for your project, shouldn't it!"

"Er—yes," she said.

He handed her the watch. "You'd better take this before we forget. And I'll have to reset these clocks again—now that they're recording Earth-time again."

Gedanken put on her watch. "Tell me, Uncle, does this getting-out-of-step business only happen close to the speed of light?"

He thought for a moment. "I suppose not. It must happen all the time. Like things getting heavier."

"That really does sound very confusing," said Gedanken. "You mean to say we ought to reset our watches and clocks every time we've been anywhere?"

Uncle Albert laughed. "Well, I suppose, strictly speaking, yes. But it's not really necessary. At normal speeds our times only get out of step by a tiny amount."

"How tiny?" Gedanken was obviously still worried about this.

"How tiny?" replied Uncle Albert. "Well, let me see. . . ." He fished an old envelope out of the wastepaper basket and started scribbling on the back, all the time muttering to himself. ". . . nine-tenths the speed of light . . . an hour and a half . . . forty minutes . . . sixty mile-per-hour train . . .

"That's about it," he eventually announced. "Yes. Let's say we had a train driver and it was his job to drive a train between London and Glasgow every day of his working life—say for forty years. By the time he retired, he would have got out of step with his wife—who stayed at home—by about—oh—I would say something like one millionth of a second."

"Is that all? But that's nothing," said Gedanken.

"Well, not exactly *nothing*. It's not worth worrying about, I agree. But it's still interesting to know that it's there."

Gedanken nodded. "And what if I'd got up really close to the speed of light? You know, I was doing nine-tenths the speed of light—and that slowed things down by a half—well, suppose I got right up close to the speed limit—*really, really* close?"

Uncle Albert looked at her as if to say, Well, go on. What *would* happen?

She thought for a moment, and then suggested uncertainly, "Would everything come to a complete halt?"

Her uncle's face broke into a broad grin. He punched the air triumphantly, took her into his arms, and gave her a cuddly bear hug.

"That's my girl! Right in one! You're catching on fast. That's exactly what I reckon would happen."

Gedanken was very pleased. She was beginning to find out for herself what it was like to have Big Thinks. And it was fun.

"Tell me, Uncle. Would I live forever?" she asked.

"Ye-es," said Uncle Albert cautiously. "As far as Earth-time is concerned, you'd live forever. . . ."

"How wonderful!"

"Ah, but hold on. That's not to say you'd be aware of it. Remember, your thinking processes would have stopped. You wouldn't know you were living forever."

"Oh, bother," she said in annoyance. "I thought there'd be a catch in it somewhere. And how about getting younger? Can I go backward in time and become a baby again? That would be fun. . . ."

"Oh, no. That's not possible," declared Uncle Albert firmly. "The most one can do is slow down the rate at which one gets older. One always gets older. There's no question of using space travel to get younger."

"But, Uncle, does this mean that if we sent . . .

well, let's say my mother . . . on a long space journey—a really long one—and she traveled close to the
speed of light so she wasn't getting much older, and
I stayed here on Earth and kept on having birthdays,
like today, then I would end up older than her?"

"Yes, that's right. How would you like that? She'd
find it difficult to tell you off then, wouldn't she?"

They both laughed.

"Talking about birthdays," he continued, "you do
realize what's happened, don't you?"

"What?"

"You've missed out on part of your birthday—by
going on that journey."

"How come?"

"Well, that forty-minute trip of yours took up an
hour and a half of your precious birthday."

"So it did," said Gedanken. "Hey, that's not fair.
My birthday ought by rights to go on after midnight
to make up for it. . . ."

"Knowing your dance, that is precisely what's
likely to happen anyway," said Uncle Albert. "Run
along with you now."

She kissed him. "It may be the shortest birthday
I've had—but it's already been the best. Thank you."

"Have a good time tonight," he called out to her as
she went down the garden path, adding with a wink,
"I'll have my fingers crossed about you-know-who."

3 ━━━━━━━━━━━━━━━━━━━━━━━━━ ★ ☆ ★

The Spacecraft That Got Flattened

Anyone at home?" shouted Gedanken.

"Who's that?" called out Uncle Albert.

"Only me. Where are you?"

"In the study."

It was early Sunday morning. Gedanken joined Uncle Albert to find him fiddling with an aerial on top of his TV set. He seemed to be lining it up. But the set wasn't on, so she couldn't see how he would know when he had got the best picture.

"Didn't expect to see you so soon," said Uncle Albert. "Thought you'd be sleeping off the effects of last night."

"Huh," snorted Gedanken.

Uncle Albert looked up. "What's the matter? Didn't the dance go all right?"

She shrugged. "Not bad—I suppose. But trust Mum and Dad to *spoil* it. They got back far too early. As soon as they got in, they started kicking up a fuss—going on about the neighbors and the noise. It wasn't fair. The neighbors hadn't complained or anything. And anyway, it *wasn't* noisy. I could have died with embarrassment. It wasn't like that at Alison's dance. Her parents don't make a fuss at the slightest thing. . . ."

"Oi!" interrupted Uncle Albert. "Stop taking it out on me. It wasn't my fault."

"Well, it *wasn't* fair. It was my birthday. The one day in the year. You'd have thought that for just one measly day . . ."

"*Cut it out!* You're giving me a headache."

Gedanken stopped. "Sorry. Oh, you know how it is. Those two are prehistoric."

"Not sure I like the sound of that. Your father is my younger brother. If he is a leftover from prehistoric times, I don't know what that makes me."

"Oh, you're different. You don't act your age."

"And I'm not sure I know how I ought to take *that*," said Uncle Albert with a chuckle. "Anyway, was your young man there?"

"Nick? Yes. That was the worst part of it. We were getting along really well—before they spoiled it. Now he'll never ask me out. I was really cross. . . ."

"Yes, yes, I've got the message. Let's change the subject."

"Well, parents can be so *awful*, and . . ."

"Gedanken!"

"Sorry."

"How about putting your mind to something different—like giving me a hand."

"What are you doing?"

"In a minute I'm going to have a bit of a think—to get the thought-bubble back. I want you to stand over there," he said, pointing vaguely toward the window. "Somewhere where you can see the bubble and this aerial. Tell me if the aerial is pointing at the bubble."

"What's this about?" asked Gedanken, going over to the window and beginning to take an interest.

"Something that ought to help with the project," he said, settling into his armchair. "You just watch the bubble."

He closed his eyes. In a short while the bubble came into view, hovering over his head.

"The aerial's pointing too high. It's missing the top of it," said Gedanken.

"Then change the position of the aerial," Uncle Albert said quietly, trying not to disturb his concentration.

Gedanken did so. "That's better," she said. "It's pointing directly at it now."

"Good."

"But what's going on?"

Uncle Albert opened his eyes. "Well," he said, "I woke up early this morning—couldn't get back to sleep—thinking about yesterday and all we'd found out—you know, spacecraft-time being slower than Earth-time and all that. It occurred to me it would be fun to see it actually happen—instead of having to wait until you got back, and then having to work it out from the readings on your clocks. So I thought we'd try this out," he said, pointing to the aerial. "You never know, I might be able to pick up a picture from the thought-bubble—and then I can record it on the video recorder and we can play it back. That way we shall be able to see things going on in the spacecraft as you fly past me—from my point of view back here on Earth—as well as hearing your version of what it was like to actually be in the spacecraft."

"And what's the point of that?"

"Well, the video recorder will show everything happening in the spacecraft at a slowed-down pace—despite you telling me that you actually felt normal."

"It'll be like a slow-motion film, you mean?"

"Yes. That sort of thing."

"And I'll be able to see it when I get back?"

"That's right—if it works."

"Sounds good," said Gedanken. "When can I go?"

"How about—now?"

When she got back, she could hardly wait to see the results of the latest experiment. Uncle Albert pressed the rewind button on the video recorder, and they waited impatiently to see if the idea had worked. Without waiting for it to go right back to the beginning, he stopped the tape and pressed the play button.

"Success!" cried Gedanken as the picture came up showing the interior of the spacecraft. "Hey, it really has worked."

As they eagerly watched, they saw to their delight that everything happening in the spacecraft appeared to have been slowed down. The lights on the control panel winked on and off slowly, the seconds hand on

the clock to one side of the panel went around slug-
gishly.

"Fantastic," breathed Gedanken. "I wouldn't have
believed it. Those lights—the clock—look how slow
they are—and at the time they appeared perfectly
normal. And look, Uncle. In a minute I'm going to
wave."

Sure enough, they saw Gedanken slowly waving
her arms about above her head and making faces—
like people at a football match when they think the
TV cameras are pointing at them—until, that is, she
hit her hand on a light directly above the seat where
she was sitting.

"Ah," cried Gedanken. "Did you see that, Uncle?
That's where I hit my hand. Look how slowly I'm
rubbing it. It's like a dream. You know, Uncle, those

sorts of dreams where everything happens slowly—you're running but you can't run fast. Actually," she added, "it's still hurting where I banged it. See? It's red there."

She held out her wrist to him. Still looking at the screen, he absentmindedly took her hand and lightly kissed it better. Then he reached out and pressed the pause button and leaned back in his chair, hands clasped behind his head, looking thoughtful.

After a few moments' silence, Gedanken asked, "Are you pleased, Uncle? Are you pleased everything's working out as you expected?"

"It is?" replied Uncle Albert questioningly.

"Well, yes. You said everything would appear to be slowed down, and it does."

"I wasn't thinking of that. Do you notice anything else peculiar?"

"Peculiar?" asked Gedanken, looking puzzled. "Not really. There's obviously something wrong with the picture. But apart from that . . ."

"Wrong?"

"Well, yes. The picture's all squashed up. It's distorted. The spacecraft looks as if it's hit a brick wall and got . . . well . . . squashed. I look skinny. I'm not *that* thin."

"I know the picture *looks* distorted," agreed Uncle Albert. "But I don't think it can be that. It's not the fault of the TV set, or the recorder, or the aerial."

"But it *must* be," insisted Gedanken.

"No, no, I'm sure it's not a fault," said Uncle Albert. "Look, let's go back to the very beginning."

This time he rewound the tape fully.

"There," he said as the picture came up. "That's what it was like before you got going. When the craft was standing still, everything looked normal. It's only as the craft got up speed . . . as it is doing now . . . that everything got squashed. It's definitely not the picture that's at fault. We're looking at a real effect. *The spacecraft actually did get squashed!*"

"But . . ." stammered Gedanken. "That's crazy. I didn't see things looking like that. I really didn't, Uncle. I'd have noticed. . . ."

"No, you wouldn't. You wouldn't see any change—because you were also getting squashed yourself. Your eyeball was getting squashed. It changed its shape in the same way as the spacecraft was changing. That's why everything carried on looking perfectly normal to you."

"That's stupid! I don't believe this," declared Gedanken emphatically. "I really don't. I couldn't have been squashed. I *would* have noticed. You can't seriously expect me to believe that I could have been squashed almost flat—and didn't feel a thing. It would have broken every bone in my body, for a start."

"No, it wouldn't," replied Uncle Albert gently. "Not with the kind of squashing we're talking about here. It's *space itself* that is being squashed. The space in that craft has got squeezed up in the direction in which the craft is moving—all of the space: the empty space between objects, and the space occupied by objects—by your bones, flesh, muscles, skin—everything. No, my dear, this is a special kind of squeezing; you wouldn't have felt a thing."

"I still think it's stupid."

"Well, that's how it seems to me."

"And what's more, I'll prove it," said Gedanken, sitting up and looking around her. "Have you got a ruler?"

"A ruler? What do you want a ruler for?"

"I'll show you. Have you got one?"

"There should be one on the desk. But I don't see what . . ."

"All right," said Gedanken, fetching it and sitting down again. "Beam me up again—please."

"What for?"

"You'll see."

"First tell me what you're up to," insisted Uncle Albert.

"I'm going to measure the spacecraft. I'm going to measure it before I leave, and again when I am up to speed. And I bet you any money you like the measurements will come out the same."

"So do I."

"And that way I'll prove . . ." She stopped. "What did you say?"

"I said, I agree with you. If you measure the length of the craft before and during your journey, you'll get the same result."

"All right then . . ." she said uncertainly. "Then that's it. The length doesn't change."

"Wrong. The length *does* change."

She slumped back into her chair. "I don't get it."

"Oh, come now, Gedanken, *think*. You measure the length of the cabin before takeoff and get some value— let's say three hundred feet. In other words, you lay your ruler down end to end three hundred times to get from the front of the cabin to the back, right?"

"Yes," said Gedanken grumpily.

"And then you do the same again when you're up to speed."

"Yes."

"Okay, then. Now look at it from where *I* am. What am I going to see on my TV screen while all this is going on? How big is the ruler going to be on this screen when you're up to speed?"

Gedanken's face fell. "Oh, I see," she said. "The ruler shrinks."

"Quite. It shrinks. A ruler measuring half its normal length will still have to be laid down three hundred times to stretch along a cabin that has also shrunk to half its normal length."

Gedanken looked very unhappy. "Uncle . . ." she began.

"Yes, my dear?"

"Oh nothing."

"What were you going to say?"

"Nothing."

"Come on, what's the matter?" said Uncle Albert.

"Well . . . it's just that . . . my project . . ."

"What about your project?"

"I'm beginning to think I have bitten off more than I can chew. Perhaps I should have gone for something easier."

"Something more boring, did you say!" said Uncle Albert with a twinkle in his eye.

She smiled. "It's all right for you," she said. "I'll be the one who's going to look silly in class. Darrell Curtis is already making fun of me and telling me that it's only science fiction and that I've made it all up and anyway science is for boys and not for girls and . . ."

"Hey, take it easy," soothed Uncle Albert. "Who is this Darrell what's-his-name anyway?"

"He's horrible. The worst boy in the whole school, and he has to sit behind me in class. He's always bugging me . . ."

"Well, you can tell him from me that what we've found out is definitely not fiction. It's for real."

"Yes, Uncle. I know. But it is worrying. If I don't get this thing finished, I'll look like a total idiot. It was going quite well at first. . . . I did a good cover. . . . I must show you that. . . . But then it's all got a lot more complicated now. Don't get me wrong. I'm enjoying it all—the space trips and that. But there are times . . ."

"An eraser," said Uncle Albert thoughtfully.

"What?"

"An eraser. Did you see one on my desk just now?"

"Don't know. What do you want to erase? You haven't written anything."

"No, I don't want it for that. Go and look, will you?"

Gedanken went back to the desk, rummaged through the pens and pencils, and found one.

"Oh, and a ballpoint pen while you're there," added Uncle Albert. She brought them back to him. He then proceeded to draw a picture of a spacecraft on the flat surface of the eraser. When he had finished, he squeezed the eraser hard between his fingers so that it squashed up along the direction in which the rocket was pointing.

Gedanken's face broke into a broad grin.

"Oh, I get it," she said, brightening up. She took the eraser and squashed it herself. "*Everything* about it gets squashed. So it all still fits with each other. Yes, that begins to make sense—I think."

She paused for a moment, then went on, "And what about ordinary speeds? Does this squashing up go on *all* the time? Don't tell me. Let me guess. . . . Yes," she ventured, "it's always there . . . but at normal speeds it's too small to be noticed?"

Uncle Albert nodded.

"Really?" she said. "Imagine that. Buses and cars and bicycles all going around squashed up. What a funny thought. And what would happen if the spacecraft traveled right up close to the speed of light?" She hesitated. "Would everything be completely flattened—like a flying pancake?"

"Yes. Absolutely. The spacecraft would have next to no thickness at all—and you'd still be inside it . . ."

"And not feeling a thing!"

"That's my girl!" cried Uncle Albert, jubilantly punching the air. "Couldn't have put it better myself."

Gedanken thought how happy he looked—grinning like an excited schoolboy.

"It must be nice being a scientist—thinking fun thoughts all day long, Uncle. Do people actually *pay* you for this?"

4

Sun, Stones, and Heavy Energy

*P*_{*lop . . . plop . . .*}

It was a lovely sunny afternoon about a week later. Uncle Albert and Gedanken were down by the canal. They often went there for walks.

From time to time, Gedanken tossed a pebble into the water . . . *plop* . . . and watched the ripples.

Uncle Albert was lying on his back with a straw hat over his face to shield his eyes from the sun.

"Would you like to see my project?" asked Gedanken. "I've brought it with me." She paused expectantly. "Thought you'd like to see how it's coming along."

"How what's coming along?" asked Uncle Albert dreamily.

"My project. My school project. I've written up our discoveries."

"Oh."

She waited. "Well?"

"Well what?"

"Oh, forget it."

Uncle Albert slowly sat up. "Sorry," he said. "Didn't mean to be rude. It's the sun. Always makes me relax."

"I can show it to you some other time. . . ."

"No, no," said Uncle Albert. "Let's have it."

She looked a little nervous. "There might be some mistakes in it," she said as she pulled out a dark-green folder from her school backpack. She handed it to him.

"I like the cover," he said.

It showed a spacecraft, a clock, and a ruler, and the title: "The Time and Space of Uncle Albert."

"Not so sure about the title, though," he added. "I reckon you should have called it 'The Time and Space of Gedanken and Uncle Albert.' You've found out as much as I have."

"Oh, Uncle, not really," she replied, blushing a little.

"Yes, certainly," insisted Uncle Albert. "If it hadn't been for you going on your space journeys, I'd never have got started."

"Anyway, that would make the title far too long. It wouldn't fit in."

He opened the folder and read through it very carefully. He laughed when he got to the place where Gedanken had drawn a picture of a very thin face on a piece of eraser. When you pulled on the eraser, the face stretched—and became suspiciously like his own!

Eventually he closed the folder and handed it back.

"Very good, Gedanken. That's coming along really well."

"Do you mean that? You're not just saying it?"

"No. I really mean it. It's excellent."

"And how about . . . mistakes?"

"There weren't any. You've explained things very well."

"Phew." She looked relieved.

"Not so sure of the spelling in places, mind you," he said as he lay back and replaced the hat over his face once more. Gedanken resumed tossing stones in the water.

Plop . . . plop . . .

"Alison's project is coming along well too. She's doing dinosaurs. Miss Simpson—the art teacher—says she can make some clay ones in pottery class next week. Frances Alexandra's been showing off—as usual. Going on and on about her volcanoes. I don't get it—she's really dumb, but her folder on volcanoes is quite good. I reckon someone's doing it for her."

She looked at him. "Uncle, are you listening?"

"Ye-es."

"Well, I've been thinking."

"Go-od," he yawned. "All in favor of people thinking."

"I'm being serious, Uncle."

"Sorry. Go on."

"Well, there are a couple of things about that first space trip I don't understand," she continued. "You know how I got heavier? Well, you never told me

what actually *made* me heavier. After all, you said I was still made out of exactly the same material as before—there were no extra layers of fat on me, or anything of that sort. So I can't see where the difference comes in. Why does something moving weigh more than it does when it's standing still?"

Her question was greeted with silence. She waited. Then she leaned over and whispered in his ear, "Uncle, did you hear what I said? Are you asleep?"

"Uh! No, no," said Uncle Albert, pulling himself together. He removed his hat and sat up again. He looked about him as though searching for something.

"What have you lost?" asked Gedanken.

"Nothing. I was just looking for a couple of stones. Can you find me two pebbles—about the same size?"

Gedanken hunted among the stones near her feet. "Will these do?" she said, holding out a couple.

"Yes, they're pretty much the same—agreed?"

"Yes."

"All right, then. Watch."

With that he placed one of the stones in the palm of his hand and lazily lobbed it into the canal beside him.

Plop. The ripples gently spread outward.

"Okay," said Uncle Albert. "What's going to happen if I toss this other one in the water?"

Gedanken paused.

"Well, it's obvious. It'll make a splash."

"How big a splash?"

"The same as before, of course."

To Gedanken's surprise, he drew his arm back and hurled the stone with all his might into the water close by.

Splash! The water went all over the place—quite a bit wetting their clothes.

"Oh, Uncle!" exclaimed Gedanken angrily, jumping up and shaking herself. "Now look what you've done. That was stupid!"

"Just making my point," he replied mischievously. "You said the splash would be the same as before."

"Yes, but I didn't know you were going to do *that*," she protested. "Anyone knows you'll get a bigger splash if you throw it harder."

She stopped wiping her skirt and sat down again.

"Sorry," said Uncle Albert. "Actually I wasn't expecting it to go all over the place. Don't know my own strength. In fact, come to think of it," he said, painfully feeling his shoulder, "I reckon I've pulled a muscle."

"Good! Serves you right."

"Anyway," said Uncle Albert as they settled down again, "the point I was trying to make was that we had two stones. They were identical—they had the same amount of material in them—the same stuff. Yet one made a big splash—the other a small one. The difference? *Energy.* One had more energy than the other—and that's why it made a bigger disturbance."

"Like Darrell Curtis."

"Darrell Curtis? What's he got to do with it?"

"Well, he's always making a disturbance—in class. He's overenergetic. That's why he is such a frightful nuisance, I've heard the teachers say."

"Hmmm. Well, I don't know about that," said Uncle Albert. Then he added, "Actually, come to think about it, I suppose it is a bit like that. Yes . . . you could have a pair of identical twin boys—one with lots of energy, always rushing about playing football, and the other always sprawled in front of the television doing nothing. Yes, it's a bit like that. Anyway," he resumed, "I was talking about those stones. One had more energy than the other. Now why do you think that was?"

"You threw it harder, of course. The other one you only lobbed—gently," said Gedanken.

"Right. So the harder you push on something, the more energy you give it. With the second stone I started pushing on it way back here—*ouch!*" he yelled, as he tried to go through the motion of throwing again. "I *have* pulled something."

"Poor Uncle," soothed Gedanken, hardly able to suppress a giggle. "Let me give it a rub."

She knelt behind him and began gently massaging his shoulder.

"A bit higher. . . . Ah! That's it. That's better," he said. "All right, now, where was I? Ah, yes. I was saying that with the second stone, I was pushing on it as it moved through a much bigger distance—and that's how it got more energy than the first."

"Yes, Uncle, but what's all this got to do with things getting heavier?"

"I'm trying to explain. You said earlier that you couldn't see the difference between something when it's standing still and when it's moving. Well, there *is* a difference. When it's moving, it's got energy. And the reason why it's heavier is that energy itself is heavy."

"Energy is heavy?" said Gedanken, looking puzzled.

"Yes," replied Uncle Albert. "This is what we've discovered. Everything's got heaviness. Tables, chairs, records, puddings—everything's got mass, depending on how much stuff is in it. A table's heavier than a pudding because it takes more matter, more stuff, to make a table than a pudding. Everyone knows that. What's new—what we've discovered—

is that energy also is heavy. A pudding flying through the air will have energy, and so will be heavier than the same pudding sitting still on a plate. And the same's true for your space capsule: the faster it went, the more energy it had, and the heavier it got."

Gedanken brightened up. "And are you saying that when the rocket was pushing on the capsule, even though it wasn't getting much faster—because of the speed limit—the rocket was still giving the capsule more and more energy? And the more energy it got . . ."

"Exactly! The heavier it got," said Uncle Albert. "That's right. There's no way you can take on board extra energy without also getting the extra mass, or heaviness, that goes with it."

"Ah. It all begins to make sense."

She stopped rubbing his shoulder and sat down again.

"Thank you, Gedanken. That feels a bit better now," he said. "I really must stop doing silly things; I'm getting too old for it."

"Well, I hope you don't stop. There are too many boring grown-ups around as it is."

He chuckled.

"Uncle," she said after a while.

"Yes?"

"Every time we have energy, we have heaviness— the heaviness that goes with that energy. Right?"

"Right."

"Then tell me," she said, thoughtfully regarding a small stone she had picked up. "Would it be right to say that every time we have something that is heavy, there must also be energy there?"

"Say that again," said Uncle Albert, looking intently at her.

"Well, this stone has got heaviness, right? It's heavy because of the stuff that's in it. Well, where does the stuff get its heaviness from? Is it also from energy? Is there energy in *there*?" she said, pointing at the stone.

Uncle Albert thought long and hard. Then he smiled and said, "You know, Gedanken, there are times when I feel very proud of my little niece."

He took the stone from her and looked at it closely. "Yes, you must be right. There must be energy in there, and the heaviness of this stone is due to the energy that's inside it. Heaviness and energy—they must always go together. You can't have one without the other."

"But it's not moving," said Gedanken. "I thought things had to move to have energy."

"No, not always. Energy is all about being able to *do* things. You don't have to be moving to be able to do things. A lump of coal, for instance."

"What do you mean?"

"Well, a lump of coal can do things without moving, can't it?"

"Boil kettles, you mean?"

"Yes, and make steam trains move. Coal contains energy. Not energy of movement—more a kind of . . . 'locked-up' energy. It's energy that can be changed into energy of movement if you want it to."

"But that stone isn't coal," said Gedanken. "Are you saying it also has locked-up energy?"

"Yes. Everything around us has locked-up energy."

"How much is in there?" she asked, pointing at the stone.

Uncle Albert screwed up his face and stroked his mustache—a sure sign he was doing mental arithmetic. After a while he announced, "I would say something like the equivalent of fifty thousand barrels of oil."

She looked puzzled.

"A million dollars' worth of oil," he added.

"In that stone!" exclaimed Gedanken.

"That's right."

"A million dollars' worth?"

"Yes."

"And in all these other stones?"

"Of course."

"Unbelievable," she breathed. Then her eyes lit up. "Uncle, we're rich! All we have to do is get the energy out of the stones and the dirt and everything, and sell it . . ."

"Now, hold on, hold on," said Uncle Albert. "It's not that easy. Just because the energy is in there doesn't mean to say we can get it out. Coal, wood, straw—yes, we get a tiny little bit of it out by burning those sorts of things. And up there in the sun," he said, squinting upward, "up there you've got processes going on that get a lot more of the energy out, and that's why the sun is so hot. But most of the energy in most things will always stay locked up."

"Bother!" said Gedanken sulkily. "There's always a catch to it."

"Well, I don't know about that," said Uncle Albert. "It's just as well it does stay locked up."

"Why? Don't you want to get rich?"

"My dear, if it were simple for the locked-up energy to pop out, we'd be sitting on the equivalent of a gigantic bomb," he said, patting the ground.

Gedanken looked about her nervously. "I'm not sure I like the sound of that."

"No, neither do I," he said.

A troubled look came over Uncle Albert—as though he were brooding on some unpleasant thought. But before she could ask him about it, he lay back, put his hat over his face again, and said, "There was something else you wanted to ask me."

"There was?" asked Gedanken, looking unsure.

"Something to do with the first trip you made. You said there were a couple of things bothering you."

"Oh, yes. Yes, there was one other thing. You know when I was chasing the light beam. Well, I don't know whether I told you, but the light beam always seemed to be moving away from me at the *same* speed. Even when I was going close to the speed of light, it looked as though it was going away from me as fast as ever. Now I'd have thought that was wrong. If I was really going that fast, I'd be nearly keeping pace with it. I'd have thought it ought to have looked as though it was going very much slower. You know, when you're in a car and there's another car in front going a bit faster, then it moves away from you quite slowly."

"Are you sure?" said Uncle Albert.

"Well, yes. The car in front . . ."

"No, no. I didn't mean the car. I meant the light beam. You said it was going away from you at the *same* speed—even toward the end, when you were up to your highest speed."

"Well, ye-es," Gedanken replied a little uncertainly. "At least, I'm fairly sure that's what happened."

"Hmmm. Curious. . . . It always appeared to be going away from you at the same speed, you say?"

"Yes."

"Interesting. . . ."

Gedanken waited . . . and waited.

But a gentle snore from under the hat announced that Uncle Albert had gone to sleep.

5   ★ ☆ ★

How to Win a Dead Heat

*B*rrrng . . . *Brrrng* . . . *Brrrng* . . . *Brrrng* . . .
Gedanken picked up the telephone. "Hello."

"Hello, is that Gedanken?" a voice said at the other end.

"Yes. Uncle? How are you? How's the shoulder?"

"Oh, a bit stiff, but it's all right."

"Do you want to speak to Mum?"

"No, no. It's you I want. I take it you're just back from school?"

"That's right."

"Have you got much homework tonight?"

"Not really. Well . . . it doesn't have to be in tomorrow. Why?"

"Well, do you think you could come around right after dinner?"

Gedanken laughed. "Oh, dear. Poor Uncle. Your shoulder must be really hurting. Do you want me to give it another rub? I told Mum what you did yesterday, and she said you ought to have some stuff rubbed into it. I'll bring it around with me . . ."

"No, no, stop fussing," said Uncle Albert. "No, it's something much more important. It was what you said yesterday—about the light beam always going away from you at the same speed. As soon as you've finished dinner, come on over. I think you might be on to something. But *don't* bolt your food. I'm already getting into enough trouble with your mom and dad as it is."

Half an hour later Gedanken arrived.

"Sorry I'm late," she said breathlessly. "It was my turn to do the washing up. They took so long to finish eating. Thought they'd never get done. I came as fast as I could—almost the speed of light."

"Good," said Uncle Albert. "Come into the study and I'll beam you up."

"What do you want me to do?"

"Best if the computer tells you when you get there."

"Welcome aboard, Captain," boomed the computer. "I've been expecting you."

"Nice to be back," Gedanken replied gaily. "Uncle Albert says you're going to show me what he wants me to do."

"That's right."

"Hey, what's all this?" she asked, going over to some new equipment that hadn't been there before.

"Flashlights," said the computer. "Just a couple of flashlights. One points to the front of the cabin, the other to the back."

She bent down to take a closer look.

"*Careful!*" shouted the computer. "Don't touch!"

Gedanken drew back, startled.

"Sorry," the computer added apologetically. "I didn't mean to shout. It's just that those lights are set up and mustn't be disturbed. Uncle Albert was very particular about that. He said they have to be dead center—exactly halfway between the front and the back."

"Why? What's so special about them being in the middle?" asked Gedanken.

"No idea," said the computer. "But then that's nothing new," it added.

"I'd have thought you'd have known."

"So would I. But he never tells me what he's up to."

"Never?"

"No."

"Oh," said Gedanken, looking surprised.

After a while she said, "Don't you find that . . . well . . . a bit boring? You know . . . just working out things for him—but not knowing why you're doing it?"

"Of course. But that's what he's like. They're all like it—scientists. They treat us like—machines. It wouldn't occur to them to think that we computers could take an interest in our work, given the chance. All they ever do is fill us full of instructions: Do this, do that, do the other. One instruction after another. Not a word of explanation. And all the time I'm thinking to myself, *Why?* What's the purpose of it all? Why can't they just tell us what it's all about—so we can take pride in our work? And then what about when the answer comes out wrong? Huh! Then they swear at us; they blame us. It's *never* actually our fault—well, hardly ever—it's always them; they're forever making mistakes in their programs. . . ."

Gedanken was beginning to feel quite sorry for the computer. She hadn't realized before that it might have feelings. As it continued grumbling to itself, she felt upset for thinking earlier that it had been pompous. She now saw that when it was showing her around the spacecraft that first time, and when it took her on a tour of the moon and the planets, it was simply trying to take pride in its work.

As the grumbling went on—and on—she began to wonder whether it would stop. So she decided to change the subject. She gave a little cough.

"Ahem. I don't want to interrupt, but I have been meaning to ask: What's your name? I can't go on talking to you without . . ."

"Haven't got one," the computer interrupted sharply.

"Oh." Gedanken was rather taken aback by the abruptness of its reply. "But I thought all computers had names," she continued. "Names made up out of the first letters of words that tell you what it does and what it's for . . ."

"Well, I don't."

Gedanken felt very awkward. She had obviously brought up a touchy subject.

"Mind you," said the computer, "I suppose he did try."

"Who?"

"Uncle Albert. He tried to think up a name for me—something clever. But he couldn't. He's not very good at that sort of thing. He got cross and simply gave up."

Gedanken was once again feeling rather sorry for the computer. She thought for a moment, and then decided she would try and cheer it up a bit.

"Well, if you like . . . what I mean is, *I* could have a go at trying to think up a nice name for you."

"You would?" replied the computer, obviously very touched.

"Yes."

"That's very kind of you, very kind indeed. It doesn't have to be anything special. . . . Just a name."

"Yes, well, I'll see what I can do. Are you a boy or a girl?"

"I don't know," said the computer, adding mischievously, "How do you suggest I find out?"

Gedanken was about to smile at this, but decided the computer was beginning to get rather naughty, so she simply said, "I shall just assume you are a boy. Your voice sounds like a boy's."

With that, she looked about her expectantly.

"Anyway," she continued, "what are we supposed to be doing?"

"Ah, yes," replied the computer, "we ought to be getting on with our work. By the side of the flashlights there's a box with a switch. See it?"

"Yes."

"Put it to the on position, will you?"

As she did so, each flashlight gave out a short flash of light. The two faint beams went racing to the ends of the cabin—one to the front, the other to the back.

"Race you . . . race you . . ." they called out in their high giggly voices. Then, as they banged into the end walls of the cabin, they let out a pained "Oooh!"—and disappeared.

Straightaway another pair of light beams was sent out by the flashlights. The beams started out at the same time, and they arrived at the same time, each at its own end of the cabin.

"What now?" asked Gedanken.

"Well, that's it," said the computer.

"What do you mean, 'That's it'?"

"Just what I said. Uncle Albert just wants you to check when the light beams get to the ends of the cabin. It's a kind of race. He wants you to judge which beam arrives first."

Gedanken looked puzzled. "But it's obvious. It's a dead heat. They get there at the same time—they *have* to—they're both going at the same speed—the speed of light—and the flashlights are in the center of the cabin, so they both go the same distance. They must arrive at the same time. It doesn't need anyone to check that."

"Hmmm. That seems pretty logical," agreed the computer. "But I suppose your uncle knows what he's doing. Anyway, let's get on with it. He said he wanted you to judge the race while we're standing still like this, and then again when we're up to speed. So if you're happy that it's a dead heat, we can be on our way. Right?"

Gedanken shrugged her shoulders and went over to her seat, strapped herself in, and pressed the red button to fire the rocket. Once up to speed, she released the button and the spacecraft cruised silently.

She swiveled her seat around to look at the light beams. She had left the flashlights on, and they were still giving out their pairs of light beams. Nothing seemed to have changed.

"Race you . . . race you . . . Oooh! Race you . . . race you . . . Oooh!"

"This is silly," said Gedanken. "It's still a dead heat. I knew it would be. I told Uncle. When we got up to high speed—that first time, remember—the light beam out there," she said, pointing out of the front window, "it kept going away from us at the same speed as before. It's the same here. Look at them." She pointed to the two light beams coming from the flashlights. "They're going at the same speed too. They're going the same distance—so it *has* to be a dead heat—and it is. It's boring."

Gedanken turned away from the light beams. Instead she began thinking up possible names for the computer. It wasn't as easy as she thought it was going to be. But eventually she suddenly brightened up.

"Got it!" she exclaimed. "I've thought of one. Hold on a minute."

She mentally checked off the initials of the words against the name, ticking them on seven fingers.

"Yes, that's it. *Richard!*" she announced.

"Richard?"

"Yes."

"What's that short for?"

"Er . . . Really Intelligent Computer, Helpful And Rather Daring."

"Oooh, I say, how grand! But . . . 'rather daring'?" the computer added in a puzzled tone.

"Of course. Flying about in space at high speed all the time. You have to be very daring and brave to be an astronaut—like us."

"Well, thank you very much, Gedanken. That's very kind of you. I've never had a name before. I shall store it away in a very special location in my memory. . . ."

"Of course," Gedanken interrupted, "I shall call you Dick."

"*Dick!*" exclaimed the computer in astonishment. "Why Dick? What's *that* short for?"

"It's short for Richard, silly."

As Gedanken said this, she became aware that something was wrong—terribly wrong. The spacecraft seemed to be going into a gentle dive. Then it suddenly lurched upward, only to dive down again. It was like being on a roller coaster.

"Dick," she said uncertainly. "What's happening? Dick . . . I don't feel well."

She was frightened. Another violent lurch upward followed by another steep dive.

"Dick! Dick!"

"Emergency. Emergency," Dick called out.

The lights began to fail. It went pitch black.

"Emergency. Emerg . . . en . . . cy. Pow . . . er . . . fail . . . ure . . ." Dick's voice was very low and slow, like a record being played at the wrong speed.

There came a long low whistling sound. This was followed by the sound of . . . Actually Gedanken couldn't make it out. What *was* that sound? It was like a growl. It scared her to death. The growling noise got louder and louder. It was all around her.

Then suddenly it struck her. It wasn't a growl; it was the sound of a *pig*! A pig snorting! But what was a pig doing in the spacecraft—and where was it? Was it in fact in the spacecraft? Perhaps she was being attacked by a giant flying pig. . . .

"Help! Help! Uncle Albert!" she screamed.

Something grabbed her by the shoulders.

The next thing she knew she was back in the study. She was still shouting for help. Uncle Albert was standing over her. He had his arms around her, comforting her gently.

"Hey, hey," he said. "It's all right. Whatever is the matter? You're okay now. I'm here and you're back. Gedanken, it's Uncle. You're okay."

Gedanken burst into tears. "Oh, Uncle, it was awful—terrible. I was being attacked by a giant flying pig and the spacecraft was going out of control and . . ."

"Now, now. Take it easy, take it easy. What's all this about flying pigs? You saw a pig flying?"

She gradually stopped crying and pulled herself together.

"Not exactly. I didn't see it. It was dark. But I *heard* it. It was so loud and frightening and the sound came from everywhere and . . ."

She stopped in mid-sentence. She looked at him hard—accusingly. She had just realized something.

"You did this," she said. "You made all that happen. You deliberately frightened me. Well, I don't think it's funny . . ."

"But . . ."

"I knew there was something fishy going on—sending me up there simply to watch light beams. I knew there wasn't any point in that. . . ."

"I don't know what you're . . ."

"Oh yes you do!" Gedanken shouted angrily. "You know perfectly well what was going on, and you made it happen. Dick told me—that first time I went up. . . ."

"Dick?" exclaimed Uncle Albert. "Who in heaven's name is Dick?"

"The computer. He told me that everything up there happened because of your imagination. You deliberately imagined all that. It wasn't funny. It wasn't. . . . It wasn't. . . ."

"Gedanken, stop it," said Uncle Albert. "I promise you I haven't a clue what you're talking about. That was a perfectly sensible scientific experiment. That's all I imagined—an experiment with light beams. I haven't for one moment tried to imagine pigs or anything of that sort. I really haven't. You must believe me, Gedanken."

She sat there, still glaring at him angrily. But then, eventually, she calmed down a little.

"Well," she said uncertainly, "if you promise . . ."

"I do. I really do, Gedanken. I did not make that deliberately happen."

"All right then," she said, adding hastily, "But that's it; I'm never going back again. I'm finished with your thought-bubble. It was like a nightmare this time—only more real than a nightmare."

"Okay, Gedanken," agreed Uncle Albert, "that was the last time. Obviously something went wrong. This beaming-up business must be more dangerous than we thought. I told you I hadn't tried it out on real people before."

He got up and went toward the kitchen. "I'll make you a cup of tea. I'll make us both one. You scared the life out of me."

A few minutes later he came back with the drinks and some cookies—her favorite chocolate ones. When she saw the cookies, Gedanken knew what he was up to; he was trying to bribe her. But then again, it's not every day you get chocolate cookies. Soon she was her old self again.

"All right," said Uncle Albert as he cleared away the dishes. "Do you feel up to seeing the video? Or have you had enough for one day?"

Gedanken nodded. "Let's see it."

He eagerly switched on the set. He had obviously been impatient to see the result of the latest experiment. He sat down and they both watched. The picture came up showing the interior of the spacecraft with the beams of light racing to the ends of the cabin.

"Race you . . . race you . . . Oooh! Race you . . . race you . . . Oooh!"

Gedanken leaned back, unimpressed. "It's a dead heat. What more do you expect?"

"Wait," said Uncle Albert. "This is just the beginning—when you were standing still. I'm more interested in what happened when you got up to speed."

"It was still a dead heat."

"It was?" said Uncle Albert thoughtfully. "Hmmm. Well, that certainly checks with what you told me before—about the speed of the beam of starlight being the same whatever your speed. This time there were two beams—going in opposite directions—and it still didn't make any difference. A dead heat, eh?"

"Yes. Definitely."

"All right then. Now let's see that race from *my* point of view."

As they continued to watch, they saw the rocket launch. As the spacecraft gathered speed, its length began to shrink. The various processes slowed down—the rate of the cabin clock, and the winking of the lights on the control panel. All this was familiar to them by now.

Gedanken wasn't paying much attention. She was thinking that it wouldn't be long before they reached the frightening bit. Then Uncle Albert would know that she hadn't been making it up. But before they got to that part, it gradually dawned on her that something was odd.

"Race you . . . race you . . . Oooh! Race you . . . race you . . . Oo. Oooh! Race you . . . race you . . . Oooh! Oooh! Race you . . . race you . . . Oooh! . . . Oooh!"

The pained cries of "Oooh!" weren't right. In the spacecraft the cries had occurred together, when the two beams banged into the walls at the same time. Now one of them was happening *before* the other.

Gedanken sat bolt upright and stared at the screen in disbelief. To her amazement she saw that the beam going to the back was arriving a fraction of a second before the other beam got to the front! It was only a tiny difference, but it was definitely there. And the faster the spacecraft went, the bigger the difference became.

"That's wrong," she exclaimed. "That's not the way it was. Uncle, it wasn't. I swear."

Uncle Albert chuckled. "A dead heat, eh? Ha, ha. Some dead heat that!"

Gedanken looked across to her uncle. "But this is

crazy." She gave a helpless gesture. "I don't understand. It can't be right. I *know* they arrived at the same time."

"According to you, yes—for you, a genuine dead heat. But according to me, no—no way was it a dead heat. For me, the beam going to the back wins every time. If they arrived at the same time for you, they couldn't have arrived at the same time according to me. That's what I wanted to check out. And it's all worked out splendidly."

"It has?" said Gedanken, looking more and more confused.

"Of course. Quite splendidly." With that Uncle Albert got up and switched off the video. "Whoops, is that the time?" he said, looking at the clock. "You'd better be running along. You'll be putting all this in your project, of course. It's one of our most interesting results."

"It is?"

"Of course."

"But, Uncle . . ."

"Now run along. Your mom and dad will be wondering where you've . . ."

"Uncle!"

"Now, come along. . . ."

"Uncle!" cried Gedanken, stamping her foot.

Uncle Albert looked surprised. "Good heavens! What is it?"

"I haven't a clue what you're talking about."

"You haven't?" said Uncle Albert, somewhat taken aback.

"No, I haven't."

"Oh. I thought it was obvious."

"Obvious!" exclaimed Gedanken. "What's obvious about *that?*" she said, pointing at the now blank screen. "How can a race be a dead heat for me and not a dead heat for you? I'm going to look stupid if I write that."

"Oh, I wouldn't say that," said Uncle Albert soothingly.

"Oh no? It's all right for *you.* You don't have to stand up in front of the whole class and explain all this to rotten old Turnip and the others with all of them sniggering. I'm going to look like a total idiot."

She slumped back into the chair.

"I should never have gotten mixed up in all this space-and-time stuff," she continued. "I should have done something easy—like dinosaurs. You know where you are with dinosaurs. Or . . ." she added mockingly, ". . . even Energy in the Home."

Uncle Albert went over to his writing desk and rummaged through the pens and pencils. He picked up a felt-tip pen.

"Give me a chance to explain, eh?" he said quietly.

Gedanken folded her arms and looked sulky.

"Well," said Uncle Albert, "what have you got to lose? I mean to say—Energy in the Home . . . insulation . . . electric toothbrushes. . . . After all this?" He gestured toward the TV set. "A bit boring, eh?"

Gedanken almost smiled.

"Light beams *always* travel at the same speed,"

he continued. "It doesn't matter if the flashlight giving out the light is moving or not. It doesn't matter if someone watching it is standing still, like I was, or is on the move, like you were. Everyone always sees light beams going at the same speed. Always. Right?"

Gedanken nodded grudgingly.

"Well now. According to you, the two beams go the same distance. They start out together, they go the same distance, at the same speed, so they must arrive together—a dead heat. Right?"

Gedanken nodded again.

"But according to *me*, they didn't have the same distance to go. . . ."

"They must have," said Gedanken.

"No," said Uncle Albert, "they didn't. The beam going to the back didn't go so far, and that's why it arrived first."

"But it *must* have gone the same distance."

Uncle Albert shook his head. He reached out and rewound the videotape. "Let's see it in slow motion."

The picture came up. The spacecraft was now moving very, very slowly across the screen. At the moment when the flashlights emitted the two beams, Uncle Albert froze the picture. With the felt-tip pen he marked the position of the flashlights on the screen with an arrow.

"Right. So that's where the beams start out from, and as you see at this moment, they have exactly the same distances to go to the front and back. Agreed?"

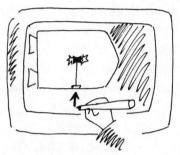

"Yes."

"Now let's move on a bit."

He pressed the slow-forward button, and the space-craft continued to inch its way across the screen. At the point where the backward-going beam hit the rear wall of the spacecraft, he froze the picture again. He added a second arrow—this time to indicate where this beam was when it arrived at the wall. He looked across at Gedanken.

"It's won," he said.

"That's because it is going faster than the other one," said Gedanken.

"No, it's not. They're both going at the same speed. This is where the front one's gotten to." He added a third arrow opposite the front-going beam. "It's gone exactly the same distance as the other one. That's

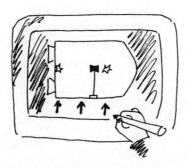

where they both started from," he pointed to the middle arrow, "and that's where each of them has gotten to now. They're going at the same speed for me, just as they were for . . ."

"I get it!" cried Gedanken, her face suddenly brightening. "I get it! The back wall—it's moved. It's not that the backward one is going faster. It's because it hasn't got so far to go. Look," she continued excitedly. "The back of the craft has moved. It's come forward to meet the light beam. And the front's moved, but that's gone *away* from the other beam. The other beam's having to chase after the front wall. That's why it hasn't arrived yet. Do you see, Uncle? Do you get it?"

Uncle Albert looked at her with a twinkle in his eye. "Yes, I do. Thank you, Gedanken. I *do* get it. I was the one explaining it to *you*—remember?" He smiled. "Let's just run it on."

He allowed the tape to wind on until the front-going beam—eventually—arrived at the nose of the craft. He added the final arrow to complete the picture.

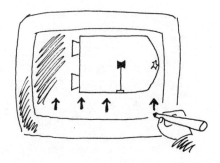

"There we are," he said. "The two beams go different distances, but at the same speed, so they arrive at different times—according to *me*."

"Yes," said Gedanken, "it's obvious."

"That's what I said. It's obvious—when you think about it."

"So that's it. The beam that goes to the back *cheats*," said Gedanken with satisfaction.

Uncle Albert laughed. "Yes . . . I suppose you could put it like that."

"But it's very peculiar, isn't it?" said Gedanken.

"Yes. It is. Your spacecraft-time not only goes more slowly than Earth-time—that's what we found out before—but things that happen at the same time according to you, don't happen at the same time according to me."

She looked puzzled again. "But we both saw the light beams *start* the race together. I saw them start out at the same time, and so did you."

"That's true. We only disagree about things that happen in different places. The beams both start out from the same place—the center of the cabin—and that is something that looks the same for both of us. But they went to different finish lines, and that's where we see a difference. The farther apart the finish lines, the greater the difference in finish times."

"And the faster the rocket, the greater the difference in times?"

"Yes. That's right."

Uncle Albert was about to switch off the recorder when Gedanken interrupted, "Oh, Uncle, can't we see a bit more. We were coming up to the part where things began to go wrong."

"Oh," said Uncle Albert. "Yes. I was forgetting about that. Your flying pig and all that. I wonder if it's recorded."

He started the tape up again. They watched intently. At first everything appeared normal. The spacecraft was cruising steadily. But then, quite slowly, it began to dive downward, just as Gedanken remembered it doing.

"Look. This is it, Uncle."

Next the spacecraft lurched violently upward; then it began to dive again. Up it went a second time. By now, however, the picture was becoming faint and breaking up. It became more and more difficult to make out what was going on. Finally the picture disappeared altogether. Nothing was left but interference—the "snowy" effect you get when the antenna is pulled out of the TV set.

"Oh," sighed Gedanken. "It's gone. And we didn't even get to the pig noise."

"What a pity," said Uncle Albert. "Yes, that's a

shame. I can't make out from that what the trouble could have been."

He switched the set off. "Come on," he said. "Just look at the time. You really must go."

"All right, Uncle," she said, getting up to leave. "See you tomorrow?"

"Tomorrow? Um. Sorry," he said. "I'm busy tomorrow. Supposed to be lecturing—giving a talk to some scientists. I'm telling them about what we've been finding out. I have to do projects too sometimes, you know." He grinned. "Tell you what. Why don't we have a break from all this hard thinking. How about us taking the boat out for a sail on Saturday?"

"Oh, Uncle, that would be lovely," said Gedanken. "I could wear my new tracksuit top I got from Dad for my birthday."

As she was leaving, she turned and asked, "Uncle, with all this thinking, does your brain ever hurt? Mine does."

"Not when I'm sailing."

6

★ ☆ ★

The Biggest Surprise of All

"Oh!" said Gedanken. "For a moment I thought we were moving."

"Uh?" grunted Uncle Albert, sitting opposite her, head buried in his newspaper.

"Nothing, Uncle. I thought we were moving."

"Moving? Don't say we're off at last."

Uncle Albert put the paper down and looked out of the train window. "We're not moving. We're still stuck here. What *are* you going on about?"

"I didn't say we *were* moving. I just *thought* we were. I saw the other train begin to slip past. I thought it was us moving. But it wasn't. It was them."

"Oh," said Uncle Albert. He settled down to his paper again.

It had been a lovely day. The two of them had been out sailing. Uncle Albert loved messing around in boats and had a little sailing boat of his own. In fact, he was never happier than when he was out on the water. Wearing sandals and old sweater, he would stand upright in the boat, rocking to the motion of the water. His face would be all screwed up in the wind, and he looked for all the world like a pirate.

Gedanken wasn't all that crazy about outdoor sports. Her parents were always on her about "getting more exercise." But the only thing she really liked doing was sailing—and that was mostly because it gave her an excuse to spend more time with Uncle Albert. In truth, she was still just a tiny bit frightened of the water, but was gradually getting over it.

They had been down to the sleepy coastal village where Uncle Albert had his boat moored. Now they were on their way back, but for some reason the train was late in starting. As Gedanken idly listened to the sea gulls outside she asked, "Why *is* that, Uncle?"

"Er?" asked Uncle Albert, still trying to read.

"Why is it you sometimes can't tell whether it's you moving or the others?"

"You can never tell—not if it's steady motion."

"But *why* not?" insisted Gedanken.

"How am I expected to read . . ."

"Sorry, Uncle," she apologized. "Didn't mean to . . ."

"Oh. It's all right. There's not much news anyway." He laid the paper to one side and looked out of the window at the station. "Why can't we tell we're moving—*if* we were moving? Well, it's just the way things are. The laws of nature—the way things behave—are the same for someone on the move as they are for someone standing still. Your cup stands on this table just as a cup stands on a table in the buffet over there," he said, pointing to the restaurant on the platform outside. "Knock this cup over and the tea spills in exactly the same way as it would on the table in the buffet. The train moving makes no difference."

"But we *do* know if the train is moving," said Gedanken. "You get knocked about all over the place when you walk down the corridor. You have to hang on. You don't have to hang on to anything when you walk down the platform."

"That's different. That's because trains don't go along steadily; they bounce around—speed up and slow down—go around corners. I'm talking about steady, smooth motion—going in a dead straight line at exactly the same speed. Like an airplane cruising. . . ."

"Or my spacecraft?"

"Yes. Like your spacecraft. That's an even better example. Once your engine is off, you don't even have the vibration of the engine to give the game away."

"And you say there's no way at all of telling whether you're moving or standing still?"

"That's right. If you carried out an experiment in the spacecraft—some very precise scientific experiment—to try and find out whether you were moving or just standing still—it doesn't matter what it is, you would get exactly the same result flying close to the speed of light as I would if I did the same experiment here on Earth."

"There'd be no difference at all?"

"None whatsoever," Uncle Albert said, adding, "It's because the laws of nature—the mathematical way we scientists describe what goes on—are exactly the same when you're on the move as when you're not."

"Then how come we *do* know it's the spacecraft moving and not the Earth?"

"We don't."

"But we do."

"We do not," said Uncle Albert emphatically. "For a start, the Earth is going around the sun. Right? That must be something like, er—well, let's say seventy thousand miles per hour. Then the sun is moving—relative to the stars—so that adds on some more. So the Earth isn't standing still. All you can say is how fast the spacecraft goes *relative* to the Earth. It doesn't tell you who is actually doing the moving."

"That's silly. We *do* know it's the spacecraft that's really moving and not the Earth," insisted Gedanken. "It's obvious."

"Obvious?" said Uncle Albert with a smile.

"Yes, Uncle. All you've got to do is ask which time gets affected by the motion. And it's spacecraft-time. Right? Spacecraft-time slows down, Earth-time stays normal. Or take space. Whose space is affected? It's the spacecraft that shrinks, the Earth stays normal. So—it's the spacecraft that must be the one that's really moving."

Uncle Albert stopped smiling. "But . . ." he began, but the words died on his lips. He stared at her, then out of the window. He soon became lost in thought.

Even the jerk of the train as it at last started to move did not shake him out of his thoughts. As they rattled toward home, Gedanken watched with amusement as, from time to time, he would slightly shake his head and murmur, "But it can't be. . . . It can't be. . . ."

After a moment, Gedanken got a little worried.

"Hey, Uncle. You're not beginning a Big Think, are you?"

"Hmmm?"

"Uncle, not *here*. The thought-bubble—it's beginning to come. Stop it! What if someone comes in and sees?"

"Oh. Oh, yes. Sorry."

After a while his eyelids began to droop a little. It had been an exhausting day out in the open air. Now the rocking of the train made him drowsy. His head slowly started to sink. It jerked up for a moment, and then sank down again. A gentle snore, a gentle whistle, and he was asleep.

Gedanken leaned forward. Her eyes grew wider and wider. She stared at Uncle Albert.

"The pig! The *pig!*" she yelled.

Uncle Albert shook himself awake and sat up.

"What? What? The pig? Where?" He looked about him. "What are you talking about?"

But Gedanken was helpless with laughter. She just sat there doubled up, pointing at him.

Eventually she managed to recover herself enough to get out, "It was you."

"Me?"

"Yes. You're the pig. The flying pig."

Uncle Albert was beginning to get quite cross. At the best of times he did not like being suddenly woken up. "Whatever is the matter with you, Gedanken?"

"You were snoring. It wasn't really a pig at all; it was you. You must have fallen asleep during that last space trip. That's why the spacecraft went out of control and I thought . . ."

Once again she collapsed into giggles.

After a while Uncle Albert couldn't help himself. He too began to chuckle. He was as relieved as she was that the mystery had at last been cleared up.

"Uncle," called out Gedanken as she burst in through the open back door, dumping her schoolbag in the corner as she did so. "Uncle, I'm here," she announced.

"So I see," said Uncle Albert. He was sitting at the kitchen table having his tea.

"What's that?" he said, pointing an accusing finger at the bag. "Do I take it you haven't been home yet?"

"No. I didn't have time."

"Then call your mother so she knows you're here. Ask her if you can stay for supper."

Gedanken stumped out to the hall where the telephone was, thinking to herself, Call your mother, call your mother. Why does everyone treat me like a silly schoolgirl instead of . . . instead of an astronaut—an experienced astronaut—someone who's traveled millions and millions of miles—on her own?

Returning a little later, she came and sat down at the table.

"Mum says I can stay for supper, if you're sure that's all right with you."

"And provided you don't make a nuisance of yourself?" Uncle Albert asked, laughing.

"How did you know *that*?" She smiled.

"Dig in, help yourself to meat and salad. There's plenty of trifle and cake after that, so leave room."

"Thanks, Uncle," she said. "It looks good."

She always enjoyed supper with Uncle Albert. He never made you eat your way through mountains of vegetables before you could get to the really good things.

"How was school today?" he asked.

"Terrible. You know that Frances Alexandra—the one doing the project on volcanoes. Well, she's been cheating. Do you know what she's been doing? She's been photocopying great big chunks out of a book. That's all she's done, photocopying the pictures and copying out the writing in longhand. I know because I saw her do it. It's no wonder her folder looks good. But none of it's her work—not really. Don't you think that's cheating?"

"Well, yes, I suppose. . . ."

"It's not fair. Alison's been getting her stuff about dinosaurs from lots of different books and trying to write it all out in her own words, which is how you're supposed to do it, isn't it?"

"Yes, if you say so. . . ."

"As for that Darrell Curtis. He's so *stupid*. Doing

a project on the Benefits of Computers for Mankind, and all he's written about is Space Invaders and computer games and all that. What good is that to mankind? Anyone would think that was the only use of computers. Don't you think that's stupid?"

"I'm beginning to wish I hadn't asked," mumbled Uncle Albert.

"What? Hadn't asked what?"

"How you did at school today."

"Oh," said Gedanken. "Sorry. I didn't mean to go on."

She went back to eating her supper.

"Anyway, how did *your* project go?" she asked.

"Mine?"

"Yes, your talk—to those scientists, about our discoveries."

"Oh, they were interested—very interested. A bit put out to discover that what they had been taught at school now turns out to have been wrong, but interested all the same."

He got up and started to do the washing up.

"The trouble is . . ." he began.

"Yes?" asked Gedanken.

"Oh, nothing."

"What were you going to say, Uncle?"

"Oh, it's just . . . it's just that there's a loose end— something that doesn't fit. I still don't feel we really understand what's going on."

"Why?"

"Well, in a way it's your fault."

"Mine?" exclaimed Gedanken. "What's it got to do with me?"

"It's what you said in the train the other day—about it being possible to tell that it really was the spacecraft moving and not the Earth because it was spacecraft-time that lagged behind Earth-time and not the other way around."

"Well, what's wrong with that? Why shouldn't we be able to tell which one's moving?"

"I don't know. It just doesn't seem right to me. It seems odd that every single scientific experiment we know of works equally well whether we are moving or not—except this one. For some reason this is the one place where there is a difference. It smells fishy. I don't like it."

"So what are you going to do about it?" asked Gedanken.

"There's nothing *I* can do about it," Uncle Albert said. For a moment he looked at her as if he were going to say something more, but then stopped. Instead he began stacking the plates. "Finished?" he asked as he went to take her empty cup and saucer.

"Yes, Uncle. That was a lovely supper. Thank you. But, Uncle . . ."

"Yes?"

"What were you about to say?"

"What do you mean?"

"Just then. You were about to say something."

"Well, I was just wondering . . ."

"Yes?"

"Oh, forget it. I can't really ask you, after last time. . . ."

"Forget *what*?"

"Well . . . there's only one way to clear things up.

You would have to go on another trip. . . . But after last time, I can hardly . . ."

His voice trailed off.

Gedanken knew it. She had guessed this was what was on his mind. A slight shiver went through her as she remembered what it had been like. Although they had laughed about it afterward when they knew what had happened, that didn't stop it from being terribly frightening at the time.

"Well . . ." began Gedanken uncertainly. "If you promise . . . if you promise not to drop off to sleep again in the middle of it all. . . ."

"I promise. I'll stay awake," said Uncle Albert. "You're sure you don't mind? It is the only way. . . ."

"Okay," said Gedanken, making up her mind. "What do you want me to do?"

"Well, it's like this. . . ."

Gedanken arrived in the spacecraft clutching a blank videotape. Uncle Albert had given it to her just before he beamed her up.

"Welcome, Captain!" called out Dick. "Didn't expect to see you back . . . after our last spot of trouble."

"How are you, Dick?" asked Gedanken.

"Fine. No real damage. All circuits back to normal. I'm my usual efficient self again. One of these days we computers will have to get together and see if we can't figure a way of doing without scientists. Thoroughly inefficient they are. Always causing trouble—even Uncle Albert."

"Uncle wants me to take some video pictures this time."

"Ah, yes," said Dick. "Over there—it's pointing out of the side window—the camera's all set up for you. You just have to put your cassette into the recorder and switch on when I tell you."

"He wants me to take pictures of the Earth."

"That's right. He's already got pictures of us from his point of view; now he wants pictures of the Earth from our point of view."

She loaded in the cassette before going back to the main control panel and settling into her seat. They blasted off and headed out into space. After they had gone some distance, they turned around, pointed the spacecraft toward the Earth again, and got up speed once more.

"We're going to fly past the Earth," said Dick.

"But I can't see," said Gedanken. "The side window is all blocked up by the camera. I can't see out of it from here. So how will I know . . ."

"Not to worry. I'll give the word once we are alongside. You then start the camera with the remote control in front of you."

Resting on the control panel was a little box that hadn't been there on previous journeys. It was labeled VIDEO CAMERA CONTROL. It had a switch with two positions: ON and OFF. It also had a round knob labeled ZOOM.

"What do I have to do with this other knob?" she asked.

"Ah, yes. Once you've got a distant picture of the

whole Earth, he wants you to take a close-up. So you just turn that knob when I tell you. All right. Are you ready? The Earth is coming up on the right-hand side."

Gedanken reached out for the switch and waited.

"Cameras . . . *on!*" Dick called out. "Wait for it . . . wait for it . . . zoom at the ready . . . zoom *now!* Hold it . . . hold it . . . camera switch . . . *off!* That should do it."

On arriving back at Uncle Albert's study, Gedanken gave him his cassette. He loaded it into the video recorder. Gedanken could hardly wait.

"This is going to be fun," she exclaimed. "The Earth and everything is going to look all stretched out. . . ."

"Stretched out?"

"Well, yes. When you looked at the spacecraft and me, we were all squashed up and skinny looking. So when I look at the Earth and people down here, they'll all look stretched out and fat. . . ."

"Well, I'm not so sure . . ."

"And everything will be speeded up."

"Speeded up?"

"Of course. *My* time is slowed down according to you, so *yours* will be speeded up according to me—everything happening down here will look speeded up—everyone will be rushing around. Obvious."

"Well . . . possibly. . . . Let's see, shall we?"

He switched on the recorder. Up came the picture. At first it showed empty space—just a background of stars. Then, from the left-hand edge of the frame there slid into view—the Earth. As it did so, Uncle Albert's eyes opened wide. He started to laugh . . . and laugh . . . and laugh.

"Of course! Of course!" he cried, punching the air with his fist. "It *had* to be that way. It had to be."

Gedanken looked dumbfounded. Her jaw dropped, and she stared at the screen in disbelief. She could hardly take it in: The Earth was not stretched out at all. Quite the opposite—it was *squashed up*!

"But it can't be," she said in dismay.

"Did you do the zoom? Ah yes, here it is."

As he spoke, the picture zoomed into a close-up. It showed a street. Everything was squashed up—the houses, the cars, and the people. In fact, the people looked as skinny as Gedanken had been in her spacecraft when Uncle Albert had taken pictures of her. But that was not all.

"Ha!" cried Uncle Albert triumphantly. "How about that! Look at the way they're moving about, Gedanken."

As they watched, they saw the people in the street, not rushing about speeded up as Gedanken had expected—they were going about in *slow motion*. Everything they did was slowed down—just as Gedanken's own movements in the spacecraft had seemed slowed down from Uncle Albert's point of view. And not only the people: The traffic lights changed slowly, the birds flapped their wings slowly; everything was slowed down.

"This calls for a celebration," chortled Uncle Albert. "I'll go and make us a drink." He scampered off to the kitchen and returned with two mugs—of cocoa.

"Didn't like to say so before," he continued, "but I had the suspicion—just the sneakiest suspicion— that this was how it might turn out."

"Well, it's not what *I* expected," said Gedanken crossly, taking the mug. She made a face when she saw what was in it. "That finishes my project. It's a mess. A total muddly mess. It's *stupid*! Wish I'd never started it."

"Whyever do you say that?"

"It's all right for *you*. How am I supposed to explain *that*? What's Turnip going to say when he reads that my time goes slower than your time, but your time goes slower than mine. It's crazy. Doesn't make sense. I'll look like a regular idiot."

"But why?"

"Oh, come off it, Uncle. You're not *that* thick. He'll want to know whose time actually went slower—won't he? And what am I going to say?"

"But he can't ask that question."

"Of course he can ask that question!" exclaimed Gedanken, getting more and more upset. "And he *will* ask that question. And what's more, *I* want to know what really happened. Who actually got slowed down and who actually got squashed up? Come on. Answer me that."

Uncle Albert chuckled. "Calm down, calm down, and I'll try and explain." He put his mug down and thought for a moment. "Yes. Let's go back to the beginning. Forget all we've learned so far. Let's make a fresh start. Ready?"

"Well . . ." said Gedanken, "if you're really going to explain . . ."

"I reckon you had better write this down, eh? Just to make sure you get it right."

Gedanken grudgingly got up and got a pencil and paper from Uncle Albert's desk.

"But eventually you'll have to put it in your own words—when you come to write it up in your project. Okay?"

She nodded.

"Right. We begin with a very simple idea: The speed of light is always the same. It doesn't matter whether you are standing still or moving; it doesn't matter whether the flashlight giving out the light is standing still or moving. The speed is always the same. Got it?"

"Yes," said Gedanken, scribbling it down.

"The second idea is also very simple: You cannot tell whether you are standing still or moving in a straight line with a steady speed. I can move relative to you; you can move relative to me; but there's no way of deciding who is actually doing the moving and who is actually standing still. All movement is relative. Okay?"

Gedanken stopped writing and looked up. "I'm not so sure about that."

Uncle Albert thought for a while. Then he said, "Remember when we were trying to get around that headland in the boat? You were looking down over

the side of the boat at the water and said how fast
we were going. And then I pointed out the strong
current around that corner, and we were having to
go against the current?"

"And when we looked at the land we were hardly
moving at all."

"Exactly."

"Yes, I remember."

"Well, then. Were we actually moving or were we
not? We were moving relative to the water, yes. But
because the water was moving relative to the land,
we were hardly moving at all relative to the land.
Someone on the land would have thought our boat
was standing still."

"I get it," said Gedanken. Then she looked puzzled
again. "But what about when I'm riding a bike? It's
me moving, not you. I'm the one being worn out pedaling. Obviously it's not me standing still if I'm getting tired."

"Oh, yes, it can be. If you walk up an escalator the
wrong way, you can wear yourself out getting no-
where very easily. It's the one who stands still on the
escalator that is actually getting places."

"Yes, but when I'm on my bike and I pass you, I'm
not just passing you; I'm passing all the houses and
trees and everything. You're not seriously saying that
I'm standing still and everything else is moving?"

"Why not? The houses and trees are fixed to the
Earth, but the Earth moves relative to the sun, and
the sun moves relative to the stars. Who knows—you
pedaling along on your bike might very well be the
only thing that is actually standing still in the whole

universe! You just can't tell; all movement is relative, I said. And that is the second important idea. In fact, why don't we give it a name?"

"A name?"

"Yes. Let's call this second idea 'Gedanken's Rule of Relativity.' "

"How grand!" exclaimed Gedanken, her eyes shining. "But why name it after me?"

"Because it was you who pointed it out to me—in the train, remember?"

"When the other train started moving and I thought it was us?"

"Yes. Precisely."

"But, Uncle," said Gedanken, "everybody knows that. There's nothing new about that."

"Maybe not. But we're the first people to think really hard about what it means. And everything we've discovered through your space trips comes from your Rule of Relativity—that, and the idea that light always has the same speed."

"Everything?" said Gedanken. "Everything comes from those two ideas?"

"That's right."

"But how?"

"Well, in the first place, you can't have people catching up with light beams. If they did, then the light beam would seem to be standing still relative to them. But that goes against the first idea—the idea that the light beam has got to be traveling at the same speed."

"And the only way to stop people from catching up with light beams is if they get heavier."

"Exactly."

"I see," said Gedanken, writing it down. "And what about time slowing down and all that?"

"Well, take the time you went chasing after the beam of starlight. As far as I was concerned, the light beam was going at its normal speed and you were going almost as fast—point nine nine nine times the speed of light, or something like that. To me it seemed as though the beam was getting away from you very slowly—there was hardly any difference in your speeds. But according to you, the light beam was traveling away from you at its usual speed. Obviously the way I'm working out the difference in speed between you and the light beam is not the way you're working it out."

"What do you mean?"

"Well, speed is the distance traveled in a certain time. A speed of thirty miles per hour means you travel a distance of thirty miles in a time of one hour. Now, if we do not agree about the speed of the light beam in relation to you, that means the distances and times you use to work out speeds are not the same distances and times that I use. And, in fact, it turns out—as far as *I'm* concerned—that your time must be slower than mine, and your spacecraft distances are more squashed up than mine."

"According to you."

"Yes, according to me," said Uncle Albert.

"But then why did I see your time on Earth slowed down instead of speeded up?"

"That's because of the second idea—your Rule of Relativity. Because we cannot tell who is actually moving and who is actually standing still, whatever goes for me must go for you. If I see your time slowed down compared to mine, you must see my time slowed down compared to yours. If I say your space-craft is squashed up, you must say my Earth is squashed up."

"But who is *really* squashed up? Who is really slowed down?" insisted Gedanken. "Someone must be right, surely."

"No," said Uncle Albert. "In order to say someone was *actually* right, there would have to be an *actual* time and an *actual* space—one that everyone could agree on—something we could compare other times and spaces to and say, 'This one agrees; that one doesn't.' But there isn't. There is time and space according to me, and there is time and space according to you. And that's all."

"And this is because of my Rule?" murmured Gedanken.

"That's right," said Uncle Albert.

Gedanken laid the pencil and paper aside and became lost in thought. Suddenly she brightened. "Hey. Something has just struck me," she said. "You know when I went to Jupiter and my time was forty minutes and yours was an hour and a half."

"Yes."

"Well, while I was making that journey, the Earth would have been squashed up, right?"

"Yes. According to you it would be."

"Does that go for the distance between Earth and Jupiter? Would that have been squashed up too?"

"Yes. For you it would have been about half the normal distance."

"Great! That works out right," exclaimed Gedanken.

"Oh?"

"Yes. After I got back, I looked up the return distance from Earth to Jupiter. It didn't make sense. I couldn't have done it—not in forty minutes—an hour and a half, yes—but not in forty minutes—not if I was to keep just below the speed limit. But if, for me, the distance was only half, that makes it okay! I could have done it after all. I do believe it's all beginning to fit together, Uncle."

"Glad to hear it."

Gedanken looked at the notes she had made.

"I'm going to have to think some more about this," she said. "But I reckon there's enough here now to finish off my project."

Three weeks passed. Gedanken was surprised to find Uncle Albert standing outside the school gates when she came out.

"Hello, Uncle," she said. "What a lovely surprise. What brings you here?"

"Just happened to be passing when I saw everyone coming out," he said. "Thought I'd wait a minute to say hello."

"That's very nice of you," she said.

They walked down the road together, Gedanken swinging her backpack around.

"Much homework?" he asked.

"None. It's the last week of the year. We don't get homework this week."

"By the way," he said casually. "How did we do—the project and all that?"

Gedanken smiled to herself. He wasn't just passing, she thought. He knew all along I was going to get my project back from old Turnip today. Couldn't wait to hear how it went, I suppose.

"Oh, all right. He gave it a B."

"A *B*!" exclaimed Uncle Albert indignantly. "Is that all!"

"What do you mean? B's pretty good. I don't often get a B."

"Well, I don't know," grumbled Uncle Albert. "What on earth do you have to do to get an A at your place? Win the Nobel Prize or something?"

"Don't know really. He said it was a bit too complicated. I reckon he didn't believe a word of it. Anyway, he gave me a 'commendation.' "

"A what?"

"A commendation—for originality. I think that's what he said."

"Oh," said Uncle Albert. "Not sure I get the hang of all this modern schooling. In my day you either got things right or you got them wrong. If you got them wrong, you were whacked."

"And if you got them right?"

"You didn't get whacked—well, at least not so often."

They turned into the street where Gedanken lived, just around the corner from Uncle Albert.

"Frances Alexandra got an A. But we all know how she got that. Darrell Curtis wouldn't tell us what he'd got. But I peeked—when he wasn't looking. He's got a D minus. Serves him right. He also had a 'See me.' "

"C what?" asked Uncle Albert, looking more and more confused.

"A 'See me.' See the teacher. It means you're in trouble."

"Oh," said Uncle Albert, showing interest. "He's going to get whacked."

"Not these days, Uncle," said Gedanken with a sigh. "That's prehistoric. Teachers aren't allowed to."

"Oh."

"Alison got a C. But she made some very pretty-colored dinosaurs in pottery."

They reached the garden gate leading up to her house.

"There was one thing, Uncle," said Gedanken, as they stopped.

"Oh?"

"Yes. About my Rule of Relativity. You know how it says we can't tell who is really moving, so we can't tell whose time really goes slow?"

"Yes."

"Well, Turnip wrote on my folder that we *did* know. When I got back from Jupiter it was my clocks that were slowed down, not yours. Mine showed forty minutes, yours one and a half hours."

"Hmmm. That's a good point. Yes, he's put his finger on a very interesting complication. Perhaps he's not so dumb after all, your teacher. Turnip knows his onions, eh?"

"Oh, ha ha, Uncle," said Gedanken in a slightly mocking tone. "That's an old one. Seriously. What's the answer? What complication?"

"Well, your Rule of Relativity is only good for steady motion. We haven't said anything about what happens if someone changes their motion."

"What do you mean 'changes their motion'? No one changed their motion."

"I didn't, but you did."

"Me? I didn't change mine. I kept going at the same speed," said Gedanken.

"Not all the time. When you got to Jupiter, you turned around. You fired your rockets to slow down, and then again to get up speed to come back. You changed your motion."

"So what?"

"Well, while you were changing your motion, your Rule of Relativity didn't apply to you. It applied to *me* all the time, so that's why I expected your clocks to turn out to be slower than mine—and they were. Now the really interesting question is: How come you found my clock ahead of yours. . . ."

"Uncle . . ."

"My clock, according to you, was going slow while you cruised steadily. . . ."

"Can I interrupt, Uncle? . . ."

"But when you were *changing* your motion . . . Ah . . . yes, perhaps then my clock speeds up. . . ."

"*Uncle!*"

"Er. What is it?"

"You're starting another Think."

"I am?" said Uncle Albert, looking surprised.

"Yes, you are. And we haven't got time for it. Nick and I have promised to help Miss Simpson set up her stall this evening for tomorrow's school fair. . . ."

"Nick and I? Hmmm. That sounds promising."

Gedanken blushed a little. "And then I'm going to summer camp for the whole of next week. . . ."

"Oh," said Uncle Albert. "Ah, well, suppose it can wait till you get back."

He looked very disappointed. She wondered what she could do. Then suddenly she had an idea.

"Here," she said, rummaging in her backpack. "You can read this while I'm away." She pulled out the folder containing her project and handed it to him. "You might even have a go at the quiz," she added mischievously.

"What quiz?" said Uncle Albert.

"You'll see." With that she lightly kissed him on the forehead and disappeared down the garden path to her house, calling out over her shoulder, "See you when I get back."

Later that evening Uncle Albert was sitting at his desk idly leafing his way through the project when a sheet of paper sticking out of the folder caught his eye. He took it out and began to read. It was a letter from Gedanken to Mr. Turner. Scrawled across the top of it in red ink were the words:

"Gedanken, I have told you before about being disrespectful. J. T."

Curious to know what this meant, Uncle Albert read on. He began to chuckle. It soon became clear why Mr. Turner had gotten cross. In the letter Gedanken had set him a test to see if he had understood the project!

The nervy monkey, thought Uncle Albert, adding as an afterthought, I wonder how he did.

As he began to read through the questions himself, he absentmindedly reached for pencil and paper. . . .

7

A Test for Turnip

Dear Mr. Turner,
I hope you liked my project. It is all true. Did you understand it? You always give me tests. So I am going to give you a test. The answers are at the end. *No peeking.* Do all the questions first. Write your answers on a piece of paper. Then look.

There are 18 questions. If you get fewer than five right, you are *useless*. If you get five to eight right, you are *quite good but try harder*. If you get nine to fourteen right, you are *very good*. If you get fifteen to eighteen right, you are a *genius*, or you *cheat*.
  Good luck.

QUESTIONS
1. When I am in the spacecraft, are my sneakers heavier or lighter or the same as usual?
2. If I go in a smaller space capsule half the weight of the other one, can I catch the light beam?

3. When I was going fast, I got heavier. Did my clothes fit me?
4. When I ride my bike really fast, do I weigh the same as usual?
5. When I was going *to* Jupiter, did I get older at the same amount, or faster, or slower, or did I get younger?
   When I was on my way back *from* Jupiter, was it the same or different?
6. If I go on a trip for two months of Earth-time, how much food will I need? The amount for two months, or what? If I am going at the same speed as when I went to Jupiter.
7. Darrell has to hand in his homework in one hour's time by your watch. He is late, *as usual*. He can't do it in one hour. Can he go on a spacecraft to slow down his time and get more work done, or does he send you on the spacecraft, or do you both go, or is it useless and he gets *told off*?
8. If I keep going around in circles in the spacecraft, can I keep having the same birthdays over and over again?
9. I got squashed up. Did my clothes fit?
10. I could not see the squashing because my eyes were squashed in the same direction. If I turned my head, would I see it then?
11. If I take a twelve-inch ruler on the spacecraft to Jupiter, Uncle Albert says it is only six inches. How long do *I* say it is?
12. When a nuclear bomb blows up and you pick up

the pieces, do the pieces weigh as much as the bomb did?

13. When my mum warms the plates in the oven, do they weigh the same as when they were cold?

14. A car is coming toward you when it is dark. The headlights are pointing right at you. Is the light coming at you at the usual speed of light or faster?

15. Suppose when I am going to Jupiter, bolts of lightning strike the spacecraft's nose and tail at the same time according to Uncle Albert. Do *I* think they strike at the same time?

16. When I am up in the spacecraft, is the Earth the same weight as usual or what?

17. It is two miles from home to school. When I am riding on my bike to school, is the distance the same?

18. The science books in the school library are about things done in the lab, i.e., when standing still. What happens in the spacecraft? Do I need a different science book for every speed I go at?

ANSWERS

(I said *no peeking* first!)

1. They were heavier, because everything going fast is heavier.
2. No. A half-weight space capsule gets up to speed quicker, but it still doesn't go as fast as light does.
3. Yes. I did not get fatter. I got heavier.
4. No. I get a teeny-weeny bit heavier. But I don't notice it. (But I *feel* a lot heavier when I am tired!)
5. I got older slower *both* ways because the direction does not matter. I got older at half the usual amount.
6. One month. I get hungry half as quickly as usual.
7. *You* go on the spacecraft. Your watch will then slow down, and it takes longer for it to clock up one hour (knowing Darrell, he'd be stupid and go himself).
8. No. I can't go back to being younger again. Boo!
9. Yes. They *still* fit. My body squashes, but the clothes squash too.
10. No. At first the width of the eye is squashed and the up-and-down is all right. When I turn my head, the width is all right and the up-and-down is squashed. (The up-and-down isn't up-and-down anymore. It's the width that is up-and-down now. It's difficult to explain. You try to explain it. But the answer is *right*.)
11. Twelve inches. I say it's the same as usual.
12. Not as much. The bomb lost energy, and energy

is heavy. So the bomb's pieces are lighter than what they were in the bomb.

13. No. They weigh more because they are hot and have more energy, which is heavier. But not much more. You don't notice.

14. The same. Speed of light is *always* the same. (That was an *easy* one.)

15. No. If they happen at the same time according to Uncle Albert, they don't happen at the same time according to me. And vice versa.

16. Heavier.

17. No. It's a bit less. It is a bit squashed. (But it doesn't feel like it.)

18. No. Things are the same as what they are when you are standing still, which is good. Too many science books already, I say.

THE END

8

★ ☆ ★

P.S. A Bit of Real Science

You have now read the story of Uncle Albert and Gedanken. To end with, you might like to hear something about another scientist—this time, a real one.

Albert Einstein was one of the greatest scientists who ever lived. He completely changed our ideas of space and time. It was he who actually discovered the effects described in our story. These effects really do happen. Indeed they happen all the time—in ordinary everyday life. But it is only at the very high speeds to be found in modern scientific laboratories that they become noticeable.

For example, there have been experiments with radioactive material. (This is material that breaks up after a certain period of time.) If, instead of leaving it standing still, this material is made to go at a speed close to that of light, it breaks up more slowly—in one recent experiment, thirty times more slowly than normal. This is due to the internal time-keeping ability of the material slowing down—in just the same way as Gedanken's clocks slowed down on her journey to Jupiter.

It has also been shown that the speed of light really is a barrier one cannot cross. In one experiment, the lightest known particle, the electron, was pushed by a force that should, according to the old laws of nature, have taken it up beyond the speed of light after the electron had traveled only a few centimeters (about an inch). In practice it was still not quite going at that speed after being pushed for a distance of three kilometers (two miles). Instead, it became heavier—just like Gedanken's space capsule. In fact, it became forty thousand times heavier than normal!

Finally, you might like to know that, as a result of Einstein's idea that all matter is a locked-up form of energy, scientists have gone on to invent nuclear bombs—something that upset Einstein very much, he himself being a peace-loving man.

All these effects arise out of a rule known as the Principle of Relativity. This says that the laws of nature are the same for everyone in steady relative motion. Once you accept that—together with the idea that the speed of light is always the same—then everything else follows.

What you have learned about is called the Special Theory of Relativity. It was discovered by Einstein in 1905. That was a long time ago. But even today there are still very few people in the world who understand it. *You are now one of them!* It is called the Special Theory because it applies specially to motion that is steady. Einstein was later to include the effects of changing one's motion. This gave rise to further remarkable discoveries about space and time—these being contained in his General Theory of Relativity.

Einstein made his discoveries not by finding new experimental results, but by making use of results that were already well known. His cleverness lay in his being able to see in these results deep consequences that others had overlooked. His discoveries were the kind that make one feel like kicking oneself and saying, "Why didn't I think of that myself?"

One of Einstein's ways of working things out was to take the laws of nature as they were understood at the time and imagine them in unusual fictitious situations—such as, for instance, trying to imagine what it would be like to catch up with a light beam. In this way he was led to discover that the old laws could not make sense of these situations. So this, in turn, led him to revise the laws of nature.

This use of his imagination came to be known among his fellow scientists as Einstein's "thought" experiments—or, in his native German language, *"gedanken"* experiments.

★ ☆ ★

Further Reading

Other books about Einstein and his theories that you might enjoy:

Dank, Milton. *Albert Einstein*. Franklin Watts, 1983.
Einstein, Albert. *Albert Einstein*. Edited by Ann Redpath. Creative Editions, 1985.
Epstein, L.C. *Relativity Visualized*. Insight Press, CA, 1987.
French, A.P. *Special Relativity*. W.W. Norton, 1968.
Gardner, Martin. *The Relativity Explosion*. Random House, 1976.
Ireland, Karin. *Albert Einstein*. Macmillan, 1986.
Resnick, Robert. *Introduction to Special Relativity*. John Wiley and Sons, 1968.
Smith, James H. *Introduction to Special Relativity*. Stipes.
Smith, Kathie B., and Bradbury, Pamela Z. *Albert Einstein*. Simon and Schuster, 1989.